STORIES FROM
THE UPPER BUNK

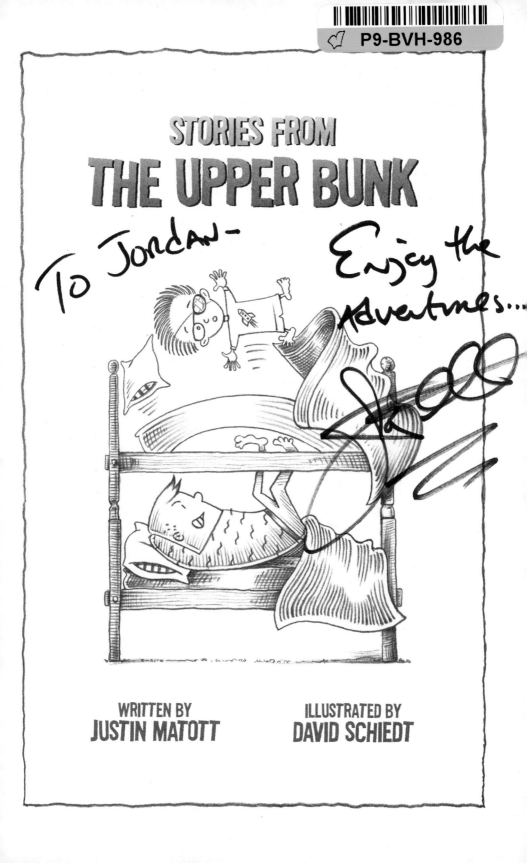

To Jordan—

Enjoy the Adventures...

WRITTEN BY
JUSTIN MATOTT

ILLUSTRATED BY
DAVID SCHIEDT

This book is based on a time when politically correct language wasn't yet in the mind of most people. There are a few references that are not in popular usage today, but they are true to the period of time in which these stories took place. Please excuse the use of words and names that are true to the stories but might be offensive in our modern day times. No insult is intended, really. Relax...

ACKNOWLEDGMENTS

To Andy Matott, the best mom I know.
Also to all the moms who have taken the time to tell me
that I am the reason their youngsters enjoys reading.
That is my mission!
J.M.
To Gail for her incomprehensible ability to stay focused for
an inordinant period of time while inputing text... more than once.
D.S.

This is a work of fiction. All names and characters are either invented or used fictitiously.
If you see someone here that you resemble, make sure it is someone you want to be.

GO ASK MOM!
STORIES FROM THE UPPER BUNK
Renewed Text copyright © 2012 by Justin Matott
Illustrations copyright © 2012 David Schiedt
Jacket design by David Schiedt
Design and Layout Buster York Creative. www.busteryorkcreative.com
Interior illustrations copyright © 2012, David Schiedt.
Jacket illustrations copyright © 2012, David Schiedt

Permissions Department, SKOOB BOOKS,
P. O. Box 631183
Littleton, CO 80163.
Library of Congress Cataloging-in-Publication Data
GO ASK MOM! written by Justin Matott.
Illustrations by David Schiedt - 1st ed. p. cm. Second Publication Edition
Summary: ISBN 978-1-889191-28-7 {1. chapter book series. I. David Schiedt - ill. II. Title
First edition / Second series
A B C D E
To contact Justin Matott regarding his work, please see his website at www.justinmatott.com.
For David Schiedt got to www.busteryork.com

Printed in China
The Four Colour Print Group

CONTENTS

YOURS TRULY, GABRIEL PETERS

"GO ASK MOM!" I screamed as my brother held the door shut to our closet, which I was currently standing in. We had been arguing for about ten minutes about whether or not I would get to use the rowboat down at the pond, which until this summer I had been forbidden to go near on account of a young girl drowning there some years back.

My brother pushed open the door and grabbed my arm, throwing me down on the carpeted floor of our bedroom. "YOU GO ASK MOM, YOU BIG BABY! YOU AREN'T GOING WITH US, AND THATS THAT!" He held me down, face first on the carpet, as he sat on my back punching me on the shoulder.

My brother was planning to sneak out the back window after dark to see if the rumors about the dead dog at the bottom of the pond were true. His dumb friend Kevin had told him you could only see the body at night, under moonlight, by flashing a flashlight directly beneath the boat as you drifted around the lake, somehow in the same way that the moon seems to follow you, the dead dog would.

"I'M TELLING HHUU!" I yelled as my big brother sat on my back pounding me. As he bounced his weight up and down on me, it forced the air out of my lungs.

"I'M TELLING!" My big brother mocked me sarcastically. "You tell and I'll whip you so bad, you'll wish you hadn't."

"I'm not afraid of you!" I yelped back, but this was a total lie. I was more afraid of my big brother than I would ever let on.

"Oh, yeah!" he mocked again, twisting my arm up behind my back.

His breath smelled like garlic and fish farts. I wanted him to get off my back. The pain in my nose was worse than the pain in my arm.

"How about a mint, butt breath?" I laughed, even though my arm hurt really badly.

I heard Mom's footsteps coming up the stairs. He jumped off me and flew to the window, taking the screen off as he hopped through, landing on the roof three feet below.

"Put the screen back on NOW! Tell Mom, Gabe, and I swear I will kick your butt good!" he snarled, looking through the window at me before crouching down low.

I could hear him dropping down onto the front porch as I slapped the screen back in place and jumped onto the upper bunk. I waited for Mom to come in, but she didn't. I must have just heard one of the dogs moving around.

Suddenly I realized that I was crying and talking to myself.

"I AM SO SICK AND TIRED OF PEOPLE PICKING ON ME!" I shouted as loud as I could into my pillow. "WHY IS EVERYONE ALWAYS MEAN TO ME?"

I don't know how long it was before I realized Mom was standing there, listening to me screaming into my pillow. She couldn't have heard what I said, but she had heard the tone. She stood next to the bunk, so near me I could smell her perfume.

I buried my face in my pillow as Mom stroked my hair and whispered to me to calm me down.

"What's the matter? Come on, tell me." Her soothing voice started to work its magic on me.

Where could I even start? Just before he had jumped out the window, my big brother Carl had punched me really hard to give me a "dead arm," something he delighted in doing. He would hit me on my shoulder muscle — what miniscule muscle there was — so hard that my arm would just hang limp. He thought this was so funny that he often demonstrated his technique in front of his two idiot friends, Kevin and Greg. So there was that.

But there was also the fact that if it was just my brother who picked on me, that would be one thing, but it seemed like everyone in the whole world thought it was great to make fun of me, trip me, punch me and, worst of all, ignore me.

Yes, I had a few friends in our neighborhood, but I never had a friend to play with on the playground at school. This was on account of the fact that my parents sent me to the only parochial school in town and sent my brother to the public school where all of the other kids in our neighborhood went because of his learning disabilities. Several days a week he went to another school for kids with problems like his. So I always had to play alone at school, except for the times I was forced to play games like dodgeball and kickball. At those times I was the last chosen, and when the teachers weren't looking the other kids picked on me.

If that wasn't enough, my best friend, Andy Epstein, was leaving for almost the whole summer. Andy was the best friend I have ever had, and when you don't have many friends, you need them around. But his family was having some big adult problems, so Andy and a couple of his brothers are going to stay with their grandparents in New York. I have never felt lonelier than I did just then, knowing that Andy wasn't going to be there to hang around with.

I couldn't really tell Mom what was the matter, but I started to cry. Mom climbed up the ladder to my bunk, and held and rocked me until the tears dried up. She asked me several times what had upset me so, but I just couldn't find the words to tell her. And I knew my brother was on the roof below our window listening in, and I wasn't going to take a chance on getting hit again by ratting on him. Still, my mother seemed to understand what was wrong.

I finally said, "Mom, someday I am going to grow really big and strong, and then no one will ever pick on me again."

She looked at me like she felt sorry for me. I could see pain in her eyes, and that made me feel bad too. I felt bad that Mom had a loser like me for a son.

CHAPTER TWO

MEET RONNIE

In fourth grade I, Gabriel Peters, was the smallest boy in my class. Worse than that, the smallest girl in the class was even bigger than me. I was what the older kids called a PEEWEE, WITH A CAPITAL P! It was bad enough to be so little, but I was really weird-looking, too.

I wore thick, black-framed glasses that looked like a giant pair of welder's goggles on my face and magnified my eyes so much that you would have thought I was some kind of an alien freak sitting in your fourth grade class. Add to that the fact that I had a lazy eye, so most of the time I had to wear an eye patch and looked like a miniature pirate-geek.

My hair also always stood up in about a hundred places, on account of my many cowlicks, so it looked like my mother had stapled a ferret to my head. Get the picture? I looked like a one-eyed pirate with a ferret, instead of a parrot.

But, worst of all, I was born with a short leg that made me walk with a limp. One of my legs was about an inch shorter than the other, so I had to wear a built-up shoe, which was a dress shoe on account of the dress code at my school. That meant I couldn't wear them outside or to play. When I outgrew the shoes or went to recess, I had to change into regular tennis shoes — P. F. Flyers. I would walk around limping as the meaner kids chanted: "Quasimodo, the pirate guy, with one bad leg, and one bad eye."

That cute little rhyme was compliments of my personal bully, Ronnie, who must have used all the wit he had to come up with something that rhymed.

In other words, I was a mess! A small, weird-looking, scared, fourth grade mess. To top it all off, I was totally terrified of my teacher, Sister Mary Claire, who seemed to have it out for me almost as much as Ronnie did. No matter what I did, she never liked me. As a matter of fact, she didn't seem to like boys too much at all, but especially me.

As I hobbled and limped down the halls of my school, the midget pirate with the bad leg, the bullies at school would seek me out to pick on me and make fun of me because of the way I looked. I sometimes laughed along like it was a great joke, but deep inside it hurt. It hurt really badly.

When Ronnie would find me in the halls, the bathroom or even in the lunch room with teachers around, he would kick the books out of my hand. He would corner me in the boy's room and push me up against the stalls, always threatening to push my head into the toilet.

The worst was when Ronnie would catch me out on the playground. He would twist my arm, kick my leg or push me down, just to make himself and a few other cruel kids laugh.

Not many days went by that Ronnie didn't pick on me. Yet I never did a thing to attract Ronnie's attentions. As a matter of fact, I did everything I could to avoid him, but somehow he always seemed to find me.

On Mondays, my least favorite thing happened: kickball. At recess, every single Monday, we would play kickball. I couldn't stand to play because I was always the last picked, and then when I would get up to home plate, I usually would miss the ball when I went to kick it because of my bad leg.

One time as I was trying to kick the ball, Ronnie ran up behind me and kicked me so hard on the back of the leg that I fell to the ground in agony as he and his friends stood pointing and laughing. On the few occasions when the mean kids got caught doing things like that to me and would get in trouble, they were just meaner to me later, as if I caused it. I always begged to stay inside during recess and clean chalkboards or anything to help the teachers, but the answer was always "NO! You need the exercise. Go out and play. Get some fresh air!"

Sister Mary Claire was the worst when I would ask her. I never understood what I did to make her dislike me so much. If I raised my hand, she ignored me, and if I didn't raise it, she complained that I wasn't listening. If I got a good grade on a quiz, she asked me if I was copying off of someone, and if I didn't do well on it, she said I wasn't applying myself. When I begged to stay in during recess, she would make mean comments about me and my leg, and say that I needed exercise more than anyone in the school. There was just no way to win with her.

But while my life seemed full of bullies, the worst bully of all was my big brother, the brother who I shared a bedroom with! Right now the good thing was, it was almost summer, and summer meant no school, and school meant no bullies except for my brother and his two sidekicks Greg and Kevin. Them I could handle a lot better than the school bullies. Or so I thought.

CHAPTER THREE

FISHIN' BUDDIES

I grew up on Venus.

I thought my life might be considered strange because of where I lived, but I didn't really have anything to base my feelings on. My life just always felt a bit odd, and I believed most kids in town had more normal lives.

My family and I lived out in the middle of nowhere, way out in the country. Some brilliant street-namer, some time way back in history, had decided to name every street in our neighborhood after a planet or something else up in outer space. So our house was at the very top of the hill on Venus, Venus Avenue. Our closest neighbors lived down the Milky Way, and others on Mars, Pluto, Mercury and Neptune. One terrible, terrifying, little old lady lived up on the highest hill on Saturn Lane.

At night where we lived it was capital D. A. R. K. The only things lighting the night sky were stars, the moon and the streetlight on the corner, across the street from our house.

Our little house on Venus sat up on the area's second highest hill, next to a gravel road leading down to the railroad tracks and some of the best fishing holes ever. There were two bodies of water that we kids spent most of our summers at, the lake and the pond. The lake was about ten times bigger than the pond and both had great swings. The big lake had huge old cottonwood trees on one side and an open field with cattails and swampy grass on the other. The tree right in the middle of the line of ten, leaned out over the lake with a great rope swing with a tire that you had to jump out to get on over the water, that sent us hurtling way out into the middle of the deep, blue water toward the raft that was anchored to the bottom, near where someone had seen the dead dog that floated around under the full moon.

But right across the gravel road from our house was the pond, considerably smaller than the lake down the hill, but it was where I spent most of my summer days catching crawdads, frogs, snakes, salamanders and other water creatures, which would come out and creep around at night.

Above the pond was this one HUGE cottonwood tree. At night in the fall and winter, when the leaves had fallen, its branches looked like long, thick skeleton arms stretching out from a huge trunk.

About fifteen feet up in that tree was our tree house. A rope swing hung under it, and when we pushed off just right, we'd zoom out over the ditch, or over the path a bit, and then fly right over the center of the pond, where we'd let go in a sort of back flip and plunge down into the water. If we didn't let go, there was the chance of coming back and slamming into the tree and getting messed up pretty badly, so even I, a total scaredy-cat, would swing out from the tree over the pond and splash down into its muddy depths where I imagined a huge sea monster was living, just waiting to pull me under.

We had a perfect view of the mountains to the west looking out over the hill that led down to a huge, open field spreading out for miles from our front yard, split by railroad tracks. Under the railroad track were three tunnels where my buddies and I spent as much time as possible in the summer. Each had flowing water, and each also had been named very creatively. They were Tunnel Number One, Tunnel Number Two, and Tunnel Number Three, called so respectively in order of their proximity to our houses. Okay, I knew they had official names, but I didn't know what the actual names were.

Each tunnel had its own individual characteristics. Number One most often sported a wild rushing creek with so many fish, bluegills, sunfish, carp and catfish that when I hung a worm off from my line, I was sure to hook into something. The water was cool, blue and clear, and I would watch crawdads crawling along the bottom and thousands of fish schooling around, running up and down the wide creek to the big lake .

Tunnel Number One provided the best skating in the winter. The water that flowed under the tunnel came out to the east and widened for a few miles along sandstone canyons, known as Fossil Creek, before it dumped into the lake where the older kids spent most of their time. We played hundreds of hours of hockey on the lake in the winter. My dad had made an insert for my skate out of one of his shoe heels, which, though it wasn't comfortable, made my left leg the same length as the other in my skate boot so I could play.

From where we sat within feet of the railroad tracks, it seemed Tunnel Number One had the shortest distance from top to bottom. We could jump from the top of One into the water safely, because it always was deep enough. So this was the tunnel where older brothers, like mine, would drag us to after tying us up from wherever they might have caught us up the hill. They would drag us down there, untying us just before hoisting us off the tunnel into the water, fully clothed.

Usually when we younger siblings were fishing off the top of Tunnel Number One and a bigger, older brother was spied heading toward us, we would take off running down the railroad tracks to continue fishing at Tunnel Number Two, where no one would dare throw anyone off on account of the fact that one time a boy jumped from there and shattered both of his legs into a billion pieces from his ankles to his hips.

Tunnel Number Two was the snake haven. Bull snakes, garters and the occasional rattlesnake slithered about in the boulder field surrounding the tunnel on both sides. The tall grass clung to the banks, and we were convinced that there were water moccasins hiding there to bite our legs as we passed through.

As to Tunnel Number Three, it was the home of a million mud sparrows that had built these tiny mud igloos which clung to the sides of the tunnel at the top. The mud sparrows would swoop down at me, like bats, when I went into the tunnel.

There were thousands of crawdads in the mud along the banks of Tunnel Number Three. Also, the biggest carp I'd ever seen was spotted lazily swimming through this tunnel.

I spent many hours fishing at all three tunnels. I would dig worms out of Dad's vegetable garden, and then hook into bluegills, carp, sunfish, the occasional trout and lots and lots of catfish.

CHAPTER FOUR
BROTHER CARL

My older brother Carl and I were adopted when we were babies from two different families. Two years separated us and we couldn't have been more different in every way, shape and size.

One night as I lay in the upper bunk, before I really understood what adoption meant, I asked Carl, "Hey, how come if we are brothers, we look so different?"

"I dunno. Go ask Mom! Go to sleep, you dumb chicken-shrimp." (My brother called me a lot of weird names, but somehow always figured out a way to include the word "chicken" in them.)

When I was in fourth grade, I was the smallest boy in my class. Carl, in sixth grade, was the biggest boy in his class. He stood well over five feet, five inches tall. He ate everything in sight, had wispy sideburns and a mustache, and was beginning to get signs of hair on his back. By the time he graduated from high school, my brother looked like a walking refrigerator with hair.

My brother was HAIRY!

My brother was SCARY!

My brother was STINKY!

My brother was DORKY!

And my brother was MEAN!

He thought it was really funny to scare me and punch me and to basically blame me for things he had messed up in the house on purpose.

One time he went out into the yard and scooped up my dog Frisky's poop. He then left it in a stinky pile on the living room floor, telling Mom that since I wouldn't let my dog out, Frisky had gone to the bathroom in the house. I had to stay in my room for the rest of the day, and Frisky had to sleep in the garage that night.

Carl was always thinking of something mean to blame on me.

Because my brother was so much bigger than me, I just had to be smarter than him. In figuring out a way to pay him back for getting me in trouble over the dog poop incident, I came up with a doozie. While he was off somewhere with his friends, I secretly pulled Carl's top dresser drawer open and took out his last two pairs of tighty-whitey underwear. Then I went down to the laundry room.

Mom always did the wash on Sunday. She then left a laundry basket with our initials on it full of our clothes that we were supposed to take to our rooms and put away in our dresser drawers before we went to school on Monday. If the baskets were there and full when Mom checked them after we had left for school, we wouldn't get our allowance that week.

I usually put my clothes away on Sunday night. Carl always waited until last thing Monday morning, when he hardly had any time to do anything in his rush to get ready for school, and so he often lost his allowance.

After dark on Sunday, I pulled out every pair of Carl's tighty-whities from his basket and put an old pair of mine in his basket. Then I snuck into Mom's sewing basket. I pulled out her sewing scissors and headed out the back door. I ran across the street and climbed up into the tree house, where I cut up every pair of Carl's tighty-whities into little shreds.

I ran back across the street and into Dad's garden to get a garden spade, then raced back across the road to bury Carl's shredded tighty-whities at the base of the cottonwood tree. I imagined tighty-whitey plants would sprout up from there one day, but they never did.

Then I snuck back across the street, put the spade and pinking shears back in their place and sat at the kitchen table across from Dad, eating my ice cream cone for dessert like nothing unusual had happened.

The next morning Carl came barreling down the stairs from our bedroom in his pajamas, as always in a mad rush. Dad's nose was buried in the newspaper, and Mom was busy making over-easy eggs and toast. Carl took a big swat at my head and then ran downstairs to the laundry room. I just chuckled silently, imagining what was about to unfold.

He jogged back up the stairs to our bedroom with his laundry basket. Within a minute he was bellowing at the top of his lungs, "MOM, WHERE ARE MY UNDERWEAR?"

"They're in your laundry basket. But they should be in your dresser by now!"

"I don't have any, Mom!"

"Don't be ridiculous. I did all of the laundry yesterday, and so they should ALL be clean!"

"But Mom, I'm telling you, I don't have any!"

"Young man, get down here and eat your breakfast right now! Stop goofing around or you will be in BIG trouble!"

"I'm not, I just..." came his plaintive wail.

"I am SERIOUS. If you don't want to be in big trouble, get dressed and get down here! You're going to be L-A-T-E!"

There was a moment of quiet before Carl rushed back down the stairs to eat breakfast. As he did so, he got a pained look on his face. "Hey, Mom, did you do all of the laundry?"

"Uh huh," she replied.

"Can underwear shrink?"

She nodded absently, "Well, maybe when it's new."

I coughed, trying not to laugh out loud.

Carl started to pull on the crotch of his pants and he looked like he was in a little pain. I just smiled and read the backside of Dad's newspaper. Carl wolfed down his eggs, groaning the whole time. He seemed to become more and more uncomfortable. Inside I was dying laughing, but I had to hold it in.

I awaited the end of the school day with an unusual amount of anticipation. I usually got home a half hour before Carl's bus came from the public school, so I rushed down the street to wait near the bus stop. I hid behind a huge cottonwood tree, knowing I could follow the ditch line, just yards away from where Carl would walk on his way home, undetected.

When Carl got off the bus, I followed behind him and his buddies, ducking in and out of the shadowy trees, watching him constantly pull on his pants and complain about how uncomfortable he was. It made me laugh so hard I almost peed my pants.

When he got home, Carl ran straight up to our room. I followed to see what he was going to do. He pulled his pants off, and then his/my tighty-whities before putting his pajama bottoms on and sighed a big sigh of relief. It was all I could do to keep a straight face, which actually I didn't, but I made some dumb excuse about hearing something funny that day. He examined the tighty-whities suspiciously and then shot me a real dirty look.

In the room Carl went through his laundry basket, and then his dresser drawer, looking for another pair of underwear again. He ran downstairs to the laundry room and looked in the washer and the dryer with a look of confusion on his face. When Mom got home he asked her if she knew what had happened to his underwear.

She didn't.

"I think I wore a pair of his underwear to school," he told Mom, shooting a look at me. "Talk about uncomfortable."

"What? He is half your size." Mom had a weird look on her face now, a kind of a smile/frown.

Don't rub it in, just stay silent, I thought.

Mom looked at me. "Gabriel, do you know what happened to your brother's underwear?"

I hated lying to Mom, and I normally didn't, but I just couldn't tell her I had shredded them all into little pieces. "Hunh?" I said, trying to look completely bewildered.

"Young man, if you know where Carl's underwear are, I strongly suggest you tell me now!"

"Oh, I, uh..."

Carl was on to me now as he snarled, "Hey chicken punk, you better tell me where they are right now or I will pound you into the ground."

At his language, my mother turned on him. "Carl, I can handle this, and I don't like that kind of talk, you know that!"

"Oh, sorry, Mom..."

She rounded on me now. "I'm waiting, Gabriel!"

My lower lip started to curl down the way it does every time I get in trouble or an adult talks to me in a tough voice. "I, uh..."

"Perhaps you would like to stay in your room through dinner and think about this more."

Somehow, I knew I wasn't getting out of this one, so I figured I might as well just get it out. I pointed at Carl as I tried to explain, "Well, he..."

"I am not interested in what he did right now, I am interested in what you did!"

"I, uh, planted them, I mean I, uh, I, buried them, and..."

"WHAT?" both Carl and my mom said at the same time.

"Well, what I mean is that I, well, you know those fruit-of-the-loom commercials?"

"What are you talking about, you chicken weirdo?" Carl growled.

"I got really mad at him, so I took all of his underwear and cut them up and planted them across the street by the tree," I sighed, knowing there was no way out of getting in big trouble now.

"WHY?" both Carl and my mom said at the same time again.

"Like I said, I got real mad!"

Mom made me take her across the road to show her. I dug down about a foot and small scraps of underwear came out of the ground with each shovel dig. Mom made a weird noise. It sounded like she was laughing in her hand, but I knew she was too mad to do that.

"Gabriel, of all of the hair-brained things to do. This one tops them all." We walked back to my yard, and Mom told me to go to my room, get my Snoopy piggy bank and meet her at the car.

I got the bank and met Mom in the driveway. As we pulled out toward town Mom told me I was spending my hard- earned money, that I was saving for a Hotwheels loop-to-loop track, on some new underwear for my dumb brother.

At Sears, I bought two three-packs of tighty-whities in my dumb big brother's size and kissed all hopes of having my own Hotwheels track goodbye.

CHAPTER FIVE
ME, A STORYTELLER?

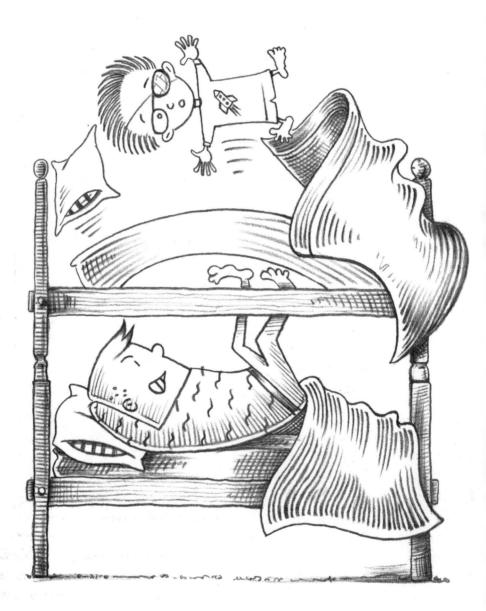

My brother's sense of humor was dark and mean. He really thought he was at his funniest when his jokes created some kind of pain for me.

When it was dark in our bedroom, my brother would hear my breath start to deepen as I began to fall asleep. Since he was down in the bottom bunk, he could place both of his feet on the bottom of my mattress and, with all the strength in his legs, LAUNCH me up into the ceiling, sending me hurtling upward as I bumped my forehead hard on the ceiling every time. This continued until I figured out that I could sleep with a pillow over my face, which at least would cushion the blow slightly.

Most nights I had a hard time falling asleep for fear that Carl would just launch me again when I began to nod off. So usually I would climb down and sneak out to the bathroom, where I slept in the bathtub.

One night Carl went a little too far. He launched me not once, but twice. I wasn't ready the second time, and didn't have a pillow over my face. My nose exploded on the ceiling, and there was blood everywhere. "Y-Y-You b-better t-turn the l-light on!" I squealed.

When he did and saw what had happened, Carl's face turned white. My whole front was covered with maroon, sticky blood. I began to stammer, "I-I-I-I'm going to g-g-o tell Mom!"

"You tell Mom and I will punch you SO hard you'll have a black eye to go with it!"

"Okay," I shuddered, "I'm g-g-going to g-go back to b-bed." "GRUNT

I lay in my bed shaking. I was shaking from the pain, and from being so mad. When I heard his breathing deepen, I sneaked down and into the bathroom and made a bed in the bathtub.

The next morning I awakened tired and mad. I was so sick of being picked on. I looked into the mirror; my whole face was covered in crusted blood. My brother was already gone when

I got up. He had gone outside, to the bus stop to play tetherball with his buddies and probably brag about how he made my nose blow up in the middle of the night.

I cleaned up the blood on my face and changed out of my pajamas then went downstairs where Dad was sitting at the kitchen table.

My dad was a really smart dad – an English professor – and he always seemed to have the answers to any problem. Dad was sitting there with his big paper spread out in the air in front of him, reading and drinking his coffee.

I sat across from him and tried to get his attention by
clearing my throat. "Ahem."

He grunted in reply.

I cleared my throat a little louder. "Ahem."

He grunted a little louder.

"AHEM!"

"GRUNT.

Finally I cleared my throat at full volume. "AHEM!"

"GRRRR... WHAT DO YOU WANT?" he boomed as his
newspaper collapsed. Then his face broke into a wide smile as
he saw me.

"Hey, Dad."

"What's up, buddy?" He ruffled my hair with his hand.

"Well, Dad, I have this probl..." I suddenly thought about
what my brother would do to me if I got him in trouble.
"Actually, I have this friend who has a problem. You see, he's
little like me, and his brother is really, really big, and always
picks on him. What can a little guy do to a big guy to get him
to stop being so mean?"

My dad took a long sip from his coffee, looked thoughtfully
at me and then asked, "Is this friend of yours as good of a
storyteller as you?"

"WHAT?" I couldn't believe my ears. What did that have to
do with anything? Who cares about storytelling when an ape is
pummeling you?

"Is he a good storyteller, like you?"

"You think I'm a good storyteller?" I was thinking that my
dad was an English professor and heard stories all the time,
and so I was surprised that he thought I could tell good stories.

"No, I think you are one of the best storytellers I have ever
heard! I mean, when you want to make people laugh, you really
can. And when you want to scare someone with your stories,
you tell really scary stories too. If you need another opinion,
go ask Mom; she thinks so too!"

"For real?" I stammered. I couldn't believe Dad really
thought I was that good.

"For real," he said.

"FOR REAL?" I said, still not believing that my dad could
think I had skills.

"For real." He looked at me proudly.

"FOR REAL!"

Dad gave me his half-serious, half-joking look, "Gabe, knock
it off!"

"Sorry." Then I thought, what does this have to do with my,
er, my friend's problem? "I mean, yeah, he tells stories like me.
Why?"

"Well, tell your friend that I said that when you don't have
the brawn, you can use the brain. I mean, sometimes if you
can make someone laugh or even scare him or her, you can
make him or her think of you differently. Tell him to try telling
a story."

I thought inside my head, that's the dumbest advice I've
ever heard. I could just see it: I am going to ask my brother, or
worse, Ronnie, as he is about to punch me if he wants to hear
a story?

I felt really frustrated. Not even Dad could help me.

I dragged my coat down to the place where our carpool met,
feeling totally defeated. If Dad couldn't help me, no one could.
Then I started to think about all of the times I had told stories
around the table at dinner. That was really the only time my
brother was kind of nice to me, because I really did make him
laugh. There were even mornings on the weekends when I was
telling Mom funny stories at breakfast and I made milk shoot
out of my brother's nose. My friends would sit in the tree house
or in the tent in our backyard glued to my every word when
I told ghost stories and stories about monsters that clomped
about at night. I always tried to imagine what would scare me
the most, and I found that worked on them too. Come to think
of it, I was always telling jokes, stories or something to get a
reaction out of those people who would give me the time of day.

Just as I was about to get in the carpool car, an idea came clattering into my brain. "Yeah, that's it! A SCARY story." I said it out loud, real loud. Everyone turned and looked at me like I was some gross, disgusting bug or something, but that was nothing new.

This monster made a first appearance in my brain, and then he began to grow. I jumped into the car, got out my Big Chief notebook and a number two pencil and began to scratch notes down on the paper as fast as my pencil would fly.

The monster went from my brain to the paper and then it was as if he was walking around the neighborhood. The other kids watched me writing furiously and must have thought I was some kind of a weirdo. I was sketching and writing and sketching more all the way to school.

By the time we pulled up to the school, my monster was HAIRY and SCARY and STINKY and MEAN. My monster had a reason for being, and I began to formulate his whole story. I worked on my story at recess, and any time I could the rest of that day. My imagination grew the whole time, so much so that when night started coming on, I felt kind of nervous, thinking about my monster clomping around in the fields and roads near my house. Somehow he was becoming real to me, maybe even a bit too real. I spent the whole evening at my desk coming up with terrifying details and spooky drawings until I started to get the uneasy feeling that the monster was right outside my window. I went downstairs where the lamps were burning bright like the fire in the fireplace and my parents were sitting in the living room talking. Ah... safe. Soon I found myself scratching in my notebook, more ideas for my monster.

That night I would be ready. My brother was really going to pay for launching me into the ceiling.

CHAPTER SIX

THE MONSTER

It was getting really dark in my bedroom, and that spooky feeling I had when the lights were out was growing inside me. I imagined creatures in the pond, and something spooky waiting in our closet for total darkness to come. For the first time I could remember in a long time, I couldn't wait to go to bed.

I got ready for bed extra fast, waiting in the upper bunk for my brother to come into our room. I could hear him across the hall in the bathroom brushing his teeth, spitting and making weird noises, trying to scare me. He knew how scared I was of the dark, even though I tried to pretend I wasn't. But tonight would be his turn to be scared, if it was the last thing I did.

"COME ON! COME ON!" I shouted into my pillow. I was afraid I might lose my nerve if he didn't hurry up. If my plan backfired and he decided to beat up on me it would be bad. His punches really, really hurt.

Finally Carl headed down the hall, the floor kind of shaking as he trudged toward our bedroom. He stood in the doorway, filling the whole space leading from our bedroom to the safety of Mom and Dad, his silhouette reminding me just how big he was. I shuddered with fear, from him and my own imagination. The hair on the back of my neck stood up. "Leave the hall light on," I pleaded.

"NO!" click. I couldn't help but smile there in the dark since I really had wanted him to turn the hall light off, so our room could be extra dark for what was coming.

Carl rumbled into our room, and when he got into the bottom bunk I held on to my mattress as the whole bed shook and tossed me around a bit when his weight settled on it. Finally he settled in.

The light from the full moon was coming through the window in a long, yellow beam lighting up our otherwise dark room. I hung my head down into his space and said, "Well, hello there!"

"GET OUT OF MY FACE, YOU CHICKEN-GEEK!" he snarled angrily.

Just before he punched me in the nose, I said, "Hey Carl, do you want to hear a really scary story?"

"You can't scare me, dork!"

"Bet I can!"

"No way, you are such a chicken-pansy. You couldn't scare anyone if you had to."

"Oh really? You wanna make a bet?" I deepened my voice as much as I could.

"Bet?"

"If I scare you, do you promise not to launch me into the ceiling tonight?"

"Don't make me mad! I can do whatever I want. I don't have to make any deals with you," he growled.

I leaned into his space and leered. "Are you chicken?"

"Yeah right, I'm really chicken of you!"

"Then make a deal!" I started to "bok bok" like a chicken.

"Shut up!"

"Hmm, I guess you are a chicken!" I whispered.

He thought for a moment, then said, "All right, deal, but I'm telling you, you can't scare me!"

"Okay, so if I scare you, you won't launch me right?"

"Fine, but you can't scare me. What do I get if you don't scare me?"

"Hmmm, I won't tell Mom that it was you that stole all of Mrs. Morris's underwear off her line and tied them to the Stoltze's flag pole last weekend."

"What? I didn't do that."

News had circulated through our little neighborhood about the thieves who had stolen Mrs. Morris's underwear. She was as mad as a hornet, and was trying to find out who it was. "Hmmm, that's not what I saw in my binoculars from the tree house."

"You tell and I will smash you into the ground!" There was a touch of fear in his voice. He knew stealing was the one thing that would really get Dad mad.

"Well, come on then. If I can scare you, you have to leave me alone tonight. If I don't then I will double-kiss swear that I will never tell, take it to the grave..."

"Okay already. I win: there's no way you can scare me, you chicken-pipsqueak!"

"So, it's a deal then?" I put my hand down in his face to shake. He smacked my hand hard, "DEAL! Just tell your stupid story!"

He couldn't see it because it was so dark in our room, but I had the biggest smile on my face right then. I began, "Well, the first thing you should know about my story is that it is 100% true."

"Yeah, right!" he said, not quite as sure of himself.

"As a matter of fact, Mom told me this story," I lied.

He growled, "Yeah right!"

I said, "Go ask Mom!"

The moon had moved further to the west and now was casting a beam right across our bunk beds, which were pushed right up against the window. As my eyes adjusted to the dark, I could see that his eyes opened a little wider. When Mom said something it was pretty serious. If he believed Mom knew about this story it would seal the deal.

"Why would Mom tell you a scary story and not me?"

"She said you would be waaaay too scared," I growled.

His breathing seemed to deepen a bit as I began.

"The other night, at the stroke of midnight with a full moon in the sky, this crazy, huge, hairy monster guy who had just escaped from the insane asylum jumped off the train right down the hill from our house." My voice was in a growling whisper to make the effect that much better.

"Yeah, right! Now I know this story isn't true!"

I leaned down, looked him right in the eye and in a singsong voice said, "GO ASK MO-OM!"

His face looked like it was turning white and he lay dead still.

"The huge, hairy dude stood up and dusted himself off. He was all scratched up from jumping off the moving train, so he was really angry. He started to walk up the hill and stopped right in front of our house, where he had caught a smell in the air. He licked his huge, chapped, bloody lips and smacked his gums. You see," I paused for the effect, "the only thing this crazy monster will eat is BIG, HAIRY, SCARY, MEAN OLDER BROTHERS!"

My brother said, "Oh, yeah, sure, now I really know you are making this whole story up. Give me a break, there's no such..."

Now in a maniacal sing-songy voice, I leaned right down in his space and growled, "GOOOO ASSSSK MOOO-OOOM!" I felt the bed start to tremble a bit and realized that my big, hairy, scary, stinky brother was down in his space huddled up as far away from the window and wall as he could get, shaking a little bit. "Oh, and I forgot to tell you something else, if I finish the story, at the last word, HE will come and he won't stop until he gets what he came for, YOU!"

"Yeah right, there's no way Mom told you that!"

"GOOO ASSSSK MO-OM." But he wasn't going anywhere.

"Tonight while we were eating dinner, it was getting dark, and I saw a shadow cross the streetlight across the street. You see, this guy is some kind of a defect. He's almost as tall as our house. And as a matter of fact, his eyes are right at the same level as our bedroom window." Our bedroom window was on the second level of our house.

"Oh, yeah right! COME ON!" Carl stammered. His voice broke as fear started to grip his vocal cords.

"Gooo assssk Mooo-oom," I answered in a scary-sounding whisper. "Anyway, as we were eating dinner, you were just about to pass me the ketch... THERE HE IS!!!!" I screamed as loud as I could, jumping off the top bunk for emphasis.

"AHHHHHH..." My BIG, HAIRY, SCARY, MEAN brother screamed like a kindergarten girl and huddled under his blanket. I jumped back up in my bunk and stifled my laughter. I couldn't believe it. I was really scaring him.

I continued with the story until he softly begged me to stop. "Seriously, I am really tired. I wanna go to sleep, so stop!"

"But there is SO MUCH more to tell, I haven't even gotten to the scariest stuff!" I leaned down as far as I could without falling out of the upper bunk. "Wait a minute. Are you scared?"

'I'm just really tired, that's all. Let's just go to sleep,' Carl said in the softest, meekest voice I had ever heard him use.

I leaned down into his space, 'You aren't aaafffrraaaaiiiddd, are you?'

'No, just tired.'

I tormented him with a few more details, then said, 'Well, okay, I can stop for now, but if I were to wake up for ANY reason, I will just finish the story and what happens at the end is almost too terrible to say out loud.'

'Okay, okay. Just go to sleep!'

I put the pillow over my face and started to act like I was falling asleep. Suddenly the bed began to move about, like it did when he was getting ready to launch me. I couldn't believe it: After all that, he was still going to launch me!

He whispered as softly as he could, 'Gabe, are you awake?'

I waited, not saying anything, and when nothing happened for a few moments I peeked down to see my BIG, HAIRY, SCARY, STINKY, DORKY brother grabbing his little pillow and his little blanket, then tiptoeing out of our room to go sleep in Mommy and Daddy's room.

I couldn't believe it. I lay in my bunk saying over and over, 'YES! I DID IT! IT WORKED!' Oh man oh man, Dad was right! Dad was a genius! I just lay up there giggling and finally fell into the best night of sleep I'd had in a long time.

I woke up the next morning feeling like I had grown three feet taller overnight. I felt like a superhero. Things were going to be different from that point on – somehow, I just knew it!

Besides, if all else failed, he knew I knew about Mrs. Morris's underwear.

CHAPTER SEVEN

RONNIE AGAIN

Somehow I, the pee-wee fourth-grade little brother, had convinced my HAIRY, SCARY STINKY, MEAN, BIG brother that my mom knew all about the insane monster now roaming our streets. I had dared him to leave his bed to go ask Mom when he doubted me, and somehow I had controlled him until he couldn't take any more and had to sleep at the foot of my parent's bed for the rest of the night. AND FOR THE FIRST NIGHT IN A LONG, LONG TIME, MY BROTHER HADN'T LAUNCHED ME INTO THE CEILING!

Living inside my brother's head now, because of little old me, was the insane monster who wanted to eat him, all because of my imagination which seemed to grow more and more with each story I told. I could use my monster whenever I needed him now, and I started to think of other monsters that might appear in our bedroom when I needed them. My monster had jumped off the train and was living out in the fields, stealing vegetables from people's gardens for his mean big brother stew. He especially wanted big brothers who pick on their little brothers, on account of the fact that my monster was picked on when he was a kid, and that's what made him so vicious today. No one knew he would grow up to be so BIG and mean, and though I too didn't plan to be mean, I was going to be BIGGER and SMARTER!

There was a strange buzzing in my head as I finished my breakfast. It was like nothing else I had experienced. I felt brave. I felt like I at last had a few answers about what to do about my personal school bully, although I didn't exactly understand that morning how my storytelling, which had scared my big brother, could work with a daytime bully at school.

But soon I would.

I headed to the bus stop, and when I got on the bus, I pulled out my Big Chief Notebook and a pencil and started scratching some ideas for other scary stories. I then found myself writing down funny things – jokes and silly scenarios that would make my few buddies laugh.

   As I walked down the hall to my homeroom, Ronnie walked
by me and stuck his foot out. I fell flat on my face, and my
notebook and other stuff spread out across the hall. A girl
helped me clean it up while Ronnie and his two friends walked
away laughing at how ridiculous I looked.

Later, I was out on the jungle gym hanging upside down, all alone at recess as usual. I heard mean Ronnie's voice as he and his friends rounded the hedge and saw me there. He walked up and scowled, "Get off my jungle gym, Peters! NOW!"

In my head, something snapped. I couldn't take it anymore - no, I wouldn't take it anymore. I jumped down and looked up at him. "You don't own the jungle gym. No one does!"

Ronnie curled up his fist, and I thought to myself, that that was the dumbest thing I ever said in my whole life.

Just as Ronnie was bearing down to punch me, I said rather loudly, "Why don't you guys like me?"

He laughed and looked at his friends. "What? Look at you. You are a total loser!"

I looked at him right in the eye; after all, he was going to hit me anyway. "I'm not a loser. You don't even know me. If you did know me, you would know that I am funny, probably the funniest person you have ever met. I'll bet I could even make someone as mean as you laugh."

Ronnie got all red in the face; he was not one who liked people to talk back to him. "YOU THINK YOU'RE FUNNY?"

"No," I practically whispered, "I know I'm funny!"

He looked at me with the meanest look I had ever seen on his face. "Then make me laugh!" he demanded, his face growing even redder.

I thought about the night before with my brother. "Okay, I'll make you a deal. If I can make you laugh, you have to leave me alone for the rest of the day."

He looked at me, his eyes full of blood-red anger. "I don't have to make deals with losers. I can do whatever I want to."

Boy, this sounded familiar. "Are you chicken?" I asked, hoping the same thing that worked on Carl would work on him.

"Chicken? Chicken of you? Don't make me laugh!" His eyes darted about nervously to his friends and then shot back to me.

"Then make the deal!" I said holding my hand in the air.

"I told you I don't have to make any d..."

"Then you must just be a chicken," I said even though I knew it would probably cost me a bloody nose or a black eye.

"Yeah Ronnie, are you chicken of this pipsqueak?" One of the mean kids he always hung around with laughed.

"Why would I ever be afraid of Peters?"

"Well, you must be if you are too afraid to make a deal with me," I said with as much courage as I could build up.

His two friends looked at each other and nodded. I could tell they were afraid of making Ronnie too mad, but also that they were starting to think that maybe he was just all talk when somebody actually stood up to him.

Ronnie looked at his friends again, seemingly embarrassed and desperate. "Fine, deal. Now make us laugh."

"So, you'll leave me alone right?" I practically yelled.

"Yeah, whatever... but you better start or I am going to beat you up anyway!"

I wasn't sure this was a good idea, and usually the things that make my family laugh the most are my stories, but I didn't think these three bullies would give me the time to really tell one right, so I pulled out my little notebook, where I was writing my own joke book, from my pants pocket. They stood there with mad faces and their arms crossed.

"What do you call a guy with two left feet?" They just stared. "Doesn't matter, if he tries to chase you, he'll just run in circles." Then I thought 'what am I doing, giving them ideas about chasing me?' They groaned.

"What do you call a guy with no arms or legs in front of your door? MATT!"

"What about the same guy on your wall? ART!" I felt so nervous, I just started firing joke after joke and got even faster when I saw a smile forming on one of their faces.

"And in your bathtub? BOB!"

"What do you call a one-legged dog? POGO!"

"What do you call a three-legged dog? PEG!" One of them snorted, which made me laugh.

"What do you call a lady with a sheep on her head? BAA BAA RAA!"

"Why did the man with a ponytail go to his doctor? HE WAS A LITTLE HOARSE!"

"What did the dummy call his pet zebra? SPOT!"

They all started to chuckle. Ronnie's usually mean face was all smiles now. Then there was another small snort from one of his goony friends, and then all three of them were laughing, and I was laughing along with them. It was the first time I could remember ever laughing on the school playground. Plus I was laughing with my personal bullies: how weird was that?

The bell rang. "Shoot, I have to go NOW! Ronnie growled. "If I am even fifteen seconds late, my parents are coming in for another conference. All three of them started to move away, but right before they did Ronnie said, "Peters, you are kind of funny," and pushed me on the shoulder, just to remind me that he was in charge, I guess. Then the three of them took off running for the building, but I heard them repeating some of the funnier parts of my jokes and laughing all over again.

That night I went into the bathroom, closed and locked the door, and practiced funny jokes and stories until I knew I had winners, just in case I needed them.

The next day at school I was out at recess. I was all alone as usual, back on the swings while the other kids ran and chased each other, laughing and having a great time. Behind me, I heard Ronnie's voice as he and a couple of his friends patrolled the playground and approached me. Ronnie looked up at me and snarled, "HEY PETERS, YOU HAVE MORE JOKES?"

"S'matter of fact, I do! Same deal as yesterday?"

He sneered at me, obviously resenting the challenge again and yet unwilling to be called a chicken in front of a bigger audience.

"Yeah, whatever, but you better be even funnier this time."

I thought I would show them how cool I was first though, and I kicked as hard as I could into my backswing. As my swing came forward, I flung myself out at the highest point. Suddenly

I was airborne like Superman, flying through the air with grace.
I spread my hands out in front of me and fell through the air
for what felt like hours. Faces were filled with awe... and then it
happened.

As I went to touch down the way I had seen the other boys
do, my bad leg let out and didn't support me. My face crunched
down into the ground with a huge thud. The world went black,
and then I saw sparks, like a million stars, inside my head. I
felt my nose let go, breaking on impact. Blood spurted from my
nose, and little pieces of gravel were stuck into the skin of my
cheeks.

Ronnie and his two friends laughed so hard their eyes filled
with tears. They all were pointing at me and laughing. Their
laughter grated on me like fingernails on a chalkboard, and all
of the anger and sad feelings inside of me from being made
fun of all the time started to come up like a volcano getting
ready to erupt.

I stood and walked right up to Ronnie, standing only about
two feet from him. I looked up at him, and before I could
control the words coming out of my mouth, I screamed loudly,
"DON'T LAUGH AT ME! I MEAN IT! I AM SO SICK AND
TIRED OF YOU GUYS MAKING FUN OF ME!"

Ronnie backed away and looked at me like he had seen a
ghost. "Jeez, Peters, calm down."

"NO! I MEAN IT! YOU CAN LAUGH AT MY STORIES AND
MY JOKES, BUT DON'T EVER LAUGH AT ME AGAIN." My fists
were curled up and everything inside of me was ready to fight,
even though I knew I wouldn't last a minute against Ronnie.

All of the kids on the playground had stopped dead in their
tracks. They couldn't believe what they were seeing. Nobody
was too close to us, but it must have been a weird sight to see
little me moving toward three of the biggest kids in our school
with my fists curled and them backing away.

Ronnie looked around nervously and then back to me. He
kind of whispered, "All right, all right, Peters. Calm down,
seriously." All three of them had stopped laughing and were

looking at me like they couldn't figure out what had come over me all of a sudden. They had been picking on me for so long, and I had been just taking it day after day. Now I was demanding that they leave me alone.

What I saw in their eyes was fear. I could hardly believe my own eyes.

I wiped the blood off of my face, picked the gravel out of my cheek and began a story. "Last year we were sitting in the lunch room and I had a remote control fart machine in my lunchbox. When the lunchroom ladies came out to wipe down the tables I pulled it out and set it next to me. One of them had just bent over to pick up some trash. She was at the next table over when I pushed the button..." They started to laugh and didn't stop as I carried on.

Right about then a crowd of kids started to gather. Not many people ever came near me on the playground as though a short leg, an eye patch and bad hair might be a catchy disease, and very few people ever purposely put themselves in Ronnie's path for fear of being his next victim. But all the same, they began to gather, no doubt wondering what was so funny.

Soon the whole crowd of about twenty kids was cracking up. They were laughing with me, not at me for a change. I liked the way that felt.

And as my story ended, Ronnie did something he had never done before. He leaned over me and put his hand on my shoulder. "Peters, you were right. You may be the weirdest-looking kid I've ever seen, but you're the funniest kid I know!" And he just walked away.

I looked at my shoulder and thought, Hey that didn't hurt! That was the first time Ronnie had ever touched me and it didn't leave a sting; I couldn't believe it.

Dad was the smartest person in the whole world. Stories were changing my life.

As I walked towards the school building I heard some of the kids on the playground repeating parts of my story and laughing.

Some of them were talking about how funny I was. It felt like I had friends at school for the first time. Boy, it felt good to feel liked.

The next Monday it was time for recess again. As I mentioned earlier, Mondays were the most dreaded days of my life. They were kickball days and I was always the last picked. That alone was humiliating, but then of course didn't do well when I got up. The boys would say things like, "Does he really have to kick? Can't he just clean the bases off or something like that?" Usually what they said wasn't even that nice. I would hover near the chain link fence, trying to hide.

When they did finally pick me, there would be a chorus of complaints: "Oh man, do we have to have him on our team again?" "Not Peters, he can't even kick the ball, let alone run!" And my least favorite, "All the girls are better than him!" I always wanted to crawl into a hole and disappear forever.

This Monday the two usual captains were standing there looking over the crowd — as if they were going to do anything different than they did every week! They would pick their friends, and then pick the girls. Then, whoever was unlucky enough to get the last gimp, would point at me for their team, not even ever saying my name like they were supposed to do.

This time, just as the first pick captain, a kid named Craig, was about to pick, Ronnie walked up and looked at him. "YOUR FIRST PICK IS GABRIEL, YOUR SECOND PICK IS ME. I'M ON HIS TEAM!"

The captain said, "No way I am picking him first!"

Ronnie curled his famous fists and sneered at Craig, "Oh really?"

Craig quickly pointed at me, picking me first.

NO WAY! I had NEVER been picked first, let alone even in the top ten. Now not only was I getting picked first, but it seemed they knew my first name!

A gasp circulated through the playground. No one could believe it, mostly me.

Then Ronnie said something even more unbelievable.

"IF ANYONE EVER PICKS ON GABRIEL, YOU'LL ANSWER TO ME! NOBODY MESSES WITH HIM, UNDERSTAND?" To show he meant it, that we were friends now, Ronnie smacked me on the shoulder.

It really hurt, but I couldn't let on. My life had just taken a big change for the better. I had gone from having my own personal bully one Friday to having my own personal bodyguard the next Monday. And from that day on, no one ever picked on me again. Instead, I told funny stories on the playground, and the kids started including me in some of their games.

About three days later, some of the cool kids found me sitting alone back near some trees on the playground. Their leader said, "Hey Peters, you got any funny stories today?"

I nodded and told them some funny stories I had made up as we ate lunch together.

Soon I had someone most every day to eat my lunch with on the warm days when we ate outside. On a few occasions, some of the kids even argued about who got to sit next to me to hear my story!

Sometimes, when someone forgot and was starting to say something mean to me about the way I looked, their friend would swat them and just say the word "Ronnie." It was a word that sent shudders up everyone's spine. And that was all it took.

Good old Ronnie.

On the last day of school that year, Ronnie came up to me and said, "Well Peters, it's been real. I'll see you 'round." He thumped my arm, but in a friendly way.

Man how times had changed. Ronnie was going on to junior high, but I was sure now that when I returned to St. Joseph's after summer break, the kids would still want to be my friends, even if Ronnie wasn't there to protect me.

SUMMER WAS FINALLY HERE! SCHOOL WAS OUT!!

That very weekend, on the corner in my neighborhood where the only real friends I had ever had played with me, my brother crowded me and punched me on the arm and told me to get out of his spot or he would pulverize me.

I whispered back, "So I guess this is a good time for me to tell your buddies how your little brother scared you so badly the other night that you went in to sleep with Mommy and Daddy."

Carl looked at me with a horrified expression. I had him right where I wanted him. The last thing my brother wanted was for his friends to find out he was scared of his little brother's stories. So, Carl let me stand in the enviable position for the game and left me alone for the rest of the time we played. I just knew things were going to change now. I was going to have the best summer ever!

When we went to bed that night, just to pay him back for all of the mean, little things he did to me that day, I began in with, "Hey Carl, I overheard Mom talking to Dad this morning about that insane dude that broke out of the asylum. They saw him standing under our window last night..."

"Yeah, right!" came a muffled response. Obviously Carl was deep under his covers.

"GO ASK M O 0-0 0 M."

"You are such a chicken-dork man! I can't sleep with you going on and on with your stupid stories! I am out of here!"

Just before he went out through our door, I mouthed the words, "Are you chicken?" and giggled into my pillow.

And from that point on whenever, I got mad at my brother, or he was bugging me in our room, I would begin to tell a scary story. My brother soon got used to sleeping in the bathtub, while I stretched out and slept like a baby night after night.

THE GHOST IN RICKY'S HOUSE

My best friend Andy left the day after school got out.
It made me really sad. Andy is the only guy who really gets me,
understands me and could care less about the stuff about me that
bugs a lot of other guys. So when he came over to say goodbye, it
was all I could do not to cry in front of him.

I would really miss him a lot this summer. Afterwards I just
stayed up on the upper bunk, thinking about what the summer was
going to be like without Andy. That's when I started to think about
this boy in my fourth grade class named Ricky, who was only in
school for about four months last fall.

Ricky was really nice to me, and the closest thing to having a
real friend at school I had ever had. One afternoon after school he
even invited me to come home with him. It was weird; he didn't
care that I was strange-looking or that none of the other kids at
school liked me at the time.

We spent the better part of the afternoon reading Andy Cap
comic books, eating snacks and melting plastic into molds of little
creatures that would fold together and attach to the tops of our
pencils in a kaleidoscope of colors. We planned to sell these pencil
toppers to our classmates and make a fortune.

Ricky lived in a huge, drafty brick house. His house was so
different than mine. My house sat out in the country collecting
dust on its sills from the constant winds that would beat our house.
His house was protected from the wind and dust: It lay in the
very center of downtown, just three blocks from the campus of
St. Joseph's School.

The house Ricky lived in was the old, spooky McGrady house.
Everyone knew it was haunted and teased him about it. But he
just told them that it being a ghost house was ridiculous. You could
tell his Mom or Dad had told him that same thing, but you could
also tell that he was kind of scared. I knew I would never accept
an overnight invitation from him to spend the night, because of the
ghosts that lived in his ancient house.

Yet one day Ricky came to school with tiny invitations his

mother had helped him make. He was inviting five boys for a birthday sleepover and I was one of them. I had made the list, and I decided to go. The other boys were much more popular than me, and I was excited that they seemed so accepting of me coming to the party.

Ricky told us that we were going to spend the night in his attic. It was his idea. He had convinced his mother that it would be okay. Then, one day when we were playing kickball at recess when he told me of how he was making a "haunted house" up there with blankets and sheets and that we would spend the night telling ghost stories, just to prove that we were braver than the other boys. He wanted me to be in on setting up a prank to really scare the guys who thought they were so cool.

The next day I made up this elaborate story about how my family was traveling that weekend to one of my dad's conferences and that I wouldn't be able to come to his party after all. I would never admit it to Ricky or anyone else for that matter, but I was really scared of sleeping in Ricky's attic. My imagination would not allow me to have any fun at all when I knew there had to be ghosts up there.

After that Ricky never talked to me. He sat with the popular boys who didn't seem to like me much, and right before he moved away started to make fun of me like all of them. I think he took it personally when I didn't go to his party, that somehow I didn't like him.

I was really sad the day he moved away because I knew somehow we could have been great friends. I wonder what would have happened if I had just been brave enough to sleep in that attic with ghosts at the old McGrady house. Sometimes it is really hard to be brave when inside you feel like a total chicken.

CHAPTER NINE

ANOTHER MONSTER

The only thing that is cool about going to St. Joseph's is that it got out two weeks earlier than the kids in the public school, and even though I started to get a little bored after two weeks with no other kids to hang around with, it was pretty cool to have my mom and dad all to myself since the college where they taught ended the same day my school did.

Summer is a cool time for all kids, but it was especially my favorite time of year because both of my parents were teachers, so they got summers off, too. That meant lots of time together, which suited me fine. Sometimes I could even talk Dad into going down to one of the tunnels with me to fish. I always knew he didn't really like fishing, but he did it anyway — for me, I suppose. During the summer Mom made us all of our favorite dishes that she didn't have time to make when she was teaching. She made rhubarb and berry cobbler from the rhubarb and strawberries Dad grew in the gardens, and she packed picnic lunches for us when we went on our adventures out in the fields. My favorite part of having Mom home, though, was when she made mint iced tea and just sat on the back patio talking about all of the places we would go someday.

Mom loved my stories, and would always ask me to tell her one. She liked my spooky stories the best, which I thought was so cool. Most moms probably don't like gross stories nor really scary ones, but my mom was always game for all of what my imagination cooked up.

With that additional practice, I got really good at making up scary stories. There was many a night in the bunk beds after that first scary story night that my brother slinked off in the darkness to sleep in our parent's room or into the bathroom tub to sleep. I just kept telling scarier and scarier stories in an effort to keep my brother from picking on me. The only problem this caused was that some of my stories were so vivid and seemingly real that I myself lay awake for hours afraid of my own imagination, actually wishing my brother were there to keep me company!

On one of those nights when I had scared my brother out of the room and had frightened myself so badly, my dogs, Frisky and Friskier, began to growl with that low growl that told me there was someone out in the yard. I shook with fear as their growling increased and they started to bark violently. I thought I would wet the bed. I moved over to the window, huddling as low in my upper bunk as I could to see who or what was down there.

A warm breeze blew on my face, but there was something different about it. There was a strange, musky scent in the air. It smelled wild and dangerous. I began to imagine that I was smelling the sweat from a wild creature like a swamp creature or a Big Foot that was coming for all of the sleeping children in our small country neighborhood. I continued to squint into the night air in my small corner of the window, hoping not to be seen, knowing it was dangerous what I was doing but not able to help myself. I had to see what it was out there that was making my dogs go nuts.

The street light across the gravel road, which lay next to the old pump, illuminated our otherwise-darkened front yard. And then I saw it. There, hanging in the tree in our front yard near my window, was the monster from the insane asylum. I was sure of it. His body was hidden behind the tree, but his face, baring long, yellow fangs and evil eyes, glowing that eerie green that eyes do when the light hits them from a flashlight, stared right at me.

My dogs were absolutely going nuts now. I tried to shush them, but they were not going to be controlled. Both of them stretched their bodies up the wall next to my bunk bed, scratching at the wall, barking wildly, trying to get nearer to the window. The blood in my veins felt like it was clogged with ice cubes.

I ducked back down below the windowsill shaking with fright, but I couldn't resist. I had to look again. But when I did, I realized the monster guy had climbed up onto our roof. I could hear him scratching along the shingles right above my room, getting closer and closer.

It was time for me to make my escape. He was only a few feet away, and soon he would be diving through the screen to get to me and suck all the blood out of my veins, leaving me lying there, drained, for my family to find the next morning.

But I couldn't move. My body was totally frozen in place. I tried to scream, but no noise would come; my throat was frozen shut. Terror filled me.

Now he was looking right in my window, his evil eyes glowing green, his pungent scent filling my room. My dogs barked and barked, running around in circles and leaping toward the window, trying to protect me. All at once my body was able to move again, the feeling returning to my hands and feet. I moved away from the window. Suddenly, his face was only an inch from mine! And the only thing separating us was the screen and the curtain I hid behind.

I rolled off the top bunk, falling to the floor. I crawled into the closet trying to call for Dad, but I still couldn't speak. My voice just didn't work, and would only squeak weakly. My dogs were going totally crazy, barking and howling and scratching up the wall, trying to get to the evil intruder before he got to me.

Somehow, the imaginary monster I had made up to scare my brother had come true, and with my brother gone, he would settle on crunching my bones and eating me whole.

Dad finally came bustling into my room to see what the ruckus was all about. He hit the light on and saw me standing in the toy box in the closet, pointing at the window and still unable to speak.

Dad saw the face in the window too, so he raced over to it, pulling the screen off and looking out the now-open window.

Suddenly my vocal chords released, and the squeaking sound became my voice again. "DAD, GET AWAY FROM THE WINDOW. THE MONSTER IS OUT THERE. HE CAME FOR CARL, BUT NOW HE'S TRYING TO GET ME!"

My dad started laughing. I must have been quite the sight, standing in my underwear in my old toy box in the closet and screaming at the top of my lungs.

'Gabriel, don't be silly. Come look at this. There's a huge raccoon on the roof under the window! No wonder the dogs are going nuts.'

The raccoon, hearing Dad's deep voice, started scrambling across the roof. As I jumped up onto the top bunk in relief, joining Dad, I watched a huge raccoon jump into a tree and disappear into the night.

I began to laugh hard, relieved to know the monster had not come to call that night. But I decided to switch to another villain in my storytelling; this one had become too real.

The next morning, as Dad was frying eggs and bacon and talking to me about our night visitor, my brother came down the stairs and looked at us both curiously. Apparently he had blissfully slept in the bathtub right through the scary night.

I winked at Dad — the kind of wink that says, 'Just go along with me on this' —and said, 'So Dad, that guy that broke out of the asylum was really on our roof last night?'

My dad's face first broke out in a big smile, which he quickly changed to one of great concern. 'Well, that's what the police said.'

'WHAT?' My big brother yelped, feeling totally left out. 'How late were the police here, Dad?'

'They stayed and searched the area for several hours. They said he is armed and dangerous!' confirmed my dad.

'WHAT?' my brother's eyes were wide open now.

'Do they have any leads on where he went?' I probed.

'They think he is still in the area,' answered my dad.

My dad was just the greatest. He should have been an actor!

'WHO ARE YOU TALKING ABOUT?' My brother stared at my dad.

'Carl, don't worry about it. It will just keep you up at night,' Dad said smoothly as he winked at me.

'WHY CAN'T I KNOW?' My brother was getting mad.

'I don't want you to get scared too.' My dad looked over at me slyly.

'COME ON, DAD! GIVE ME A BREAK! IF CHICKEN-SQUIRT CAN KNOW ABOUT IT, I CAN TOO!'

I broke in, just in case Dad blew it by not knowing about the story, 'Carl, the guy I was telling you about the other night who had broken out of the asylum was on our roof looking for you last night!'

Fear broke across his face, although he tried to pretend it didn't matter. 'YEAH, RIGHT!' My brother rolled his eyes.

Dad looked over at me, wrinkling his brow. I thought I had pushed it too far, and Dad was going to blow it for me when he began, 'Well, actually Carl...'

'GO ASK MOM!' I practically yelled, desperate for an interruption.

There was a long pause before dad said, '...actually if you don't believe us, go look at the roof right below your window. He left scratch marks on the shingles when he jumped up on the roof.'

My brother bound up the stairs and yelled from our room, 'HOLY GUACAMOLE! HE WAS HERE!' He came running back down the stairs and as he began to wolf down his breakfast I noticed his hands were shaking a little.

'Dad, any chance of me moving into your study sooner?' asked Carl.

I knew my brother wanted that room because there was no roof below the window. It would be much harder for my monster to get to him in the room across the hall, but somehow my monster would manage it, that I knew.

Carl then said, 'I just have to get away from Chicken-Gabe. He is afraid of everything and he is driving me crazy!'

At this point Mom came down the stairs in her pink bathrobe and slippers with one of those, 'what the heck?' looks on her face. 'What's all the commotion about?'

Carl quickly grabbed his stuff and ran out the front door as if he didn't want to hear one more word about it. 'BYE, DAD! BYE, MOM! SEE YOU AFTER SCHOOL! SEE YOU AROUND CHICKEN-DORK!'

I could see Carl running down the street toward the bus stop as fast as he could, his head turning as he looked behind each tree and car to make sure my monster wasn't lurking, although somehow we all knew we were protected from these things by the daylight.

With Carl gone, Dad started laughing. "Okay, Gabe, now tell me what this monster business is all about."

One of the great things about going to different schools is that I got mom and dad all to myself for a short time. "Well, Dad, remember when you told me about how stories can change things..."

I sat there and told Mom and Dad about the monster in great detail, and about how it made Carl sneak out and sleep in their room and now the bathtub. Both Mom and Dad got a kick out of it, although they said parent things like, "Well, that isn't really nice," and "You really ought to tell him the truth." But deep down, I could tell they both liked the idea that now I had a way to keep my big brother from picking on me so much.

Mom then went back upstairs with a cup of coffee to take a bath and get ready for the day. Dad was sipping his coffee and looking at the paper when he said, "You know, there is something really kind of strange that scares Carl."

"What?" I asked.

"Well, it's very weird, but he is really scared of your stuffed squirrel."

"What?" I asked, totally confused.

"He used to tell me that he thought your squirrel comes alive at night and stares at him. Now, I'm not sure, but I think he still kind of believes that. He's asked me if we can make you give it up several times."

"Seriously?"

"Yup!" And with that, Dad opened up his paper and didn't say another word.

Deeden, my little gray squirrel, had been mine since I was a little baby or something like that. He was the size of a teddy bear but a bit softer than one from the many years of him sleeping in my bed. He was pretty tattered now, and Mom had fixed him several times when his innards had spilled out. He had two big blood-red beads for eyes, and a little black nose.

I guessed it was the beady red eyes that scared my brother so much. Deeden's eyes kind of glowed at night like a real animal, the way you see a wild animal's eyes flash silver when a car light hits them. It was kind of funny, though, that a big, tough, sixth grader would be frightened of them.

Because I was growing up, I had stopped taking Deeden to bed at night. Instead, I left him on my desk, which caught the moonlight. It was the light from the streetlight across the street that made his eyes glow, which my brother could clearly see from his lower bunk.

I decided to start making up stories about my squirrel now that I knew Carl was afraid of him.

CHAPTER TEN
MEET FRISKY & FRISKIER

My family's house was full of pets. Besides my two dogs Frisky and Friskier, I had two longhaired guinea pigs which I kept in a cage in my closet. One was named Squeaky, and the other, Squeakier.

We also had two cats, one named Kitty and the other named Flop. Flop was originally called Kittier, but there's a story, to come later, about how Flop got his new name.

My first pet had been Frisky, a husky/beagle mix. He became so much more than a pet to me: he was a great friend. I got him for my sixth birthday, and he was the best birthday present I have ever received!

Friskier was a black-and-white Border collie stray who followed me home one day from the fields near the railroad tracks after I fed her several of the hot dogs I was roasting with some friends for lunch on one of our famous hikes. The sweet puppy sat at our back door for several days and nights while I begged my mom and dad to let me keep her.

To impress my mom, we gave the dog a royal name. My mom didn't really even like dogs much, but because she was all into the British Royal family and pomp and circumstance, we figured if we made her out to be like royalty Mom wouldn't be able to refuse her. So Friskier's original name was Princess Christina Anna Belle.

As Princess waited for us to adopt her, Dad refused to let me feed her, saying she would find other opportunities elsewhere as long as we didn't feed her. In fact, he said very matter-of-factly, 'Once you feed a dog,

it is VERY hard to get them
to leave, so whatever you
do, don't feed her or
she'll never leave!"

Imagine my
eyebrows raising
and a large smile
spreading across
my face as a
brainstorm hit! I of course wanted to keep the beautiful white-
and-black spotted puppy, so I went upstairs and removed the
screen from my bedroom window, then whispered, "Psst, Princess
come here!"

She looked around curiously, turning her head this way and
that as she tried to find where my voice was coming from. Then
she spotted me. Her tail began to wag furiously, and she began
to dance around and run around the yard, full of excitement.
I tossed bits of cheese, hot dogs and peanut butter sandwiches
out my bedroom window to her.

Dad started to get suspicious when he found her most times
hanging about under my bedroom window, and no longer by the
back door. I knew then I would have to be really careful.

On the fourth day since she had followed me home, I saw
something in the early morning from the bathroom window
that gave me hope. Dad was in the backyard sitting on the
grass with her, stroking her tummy as she lay on her back by
his vegetable garden. I could hear him saying "Why, you are
even friskier than Frisky! You are a sweet pooch, you know that."
Dad was smiling at her like he was falling in love, and I knew
he wouldn't be able to resist her if he just spent a little time
getting to know her.

"Good morning, Dad!" I leaned out the window looking down
on the garden.

"Morning, Gabe."

"Looks like you and Princess are getting along pretty well there."

"Yeah, yeah," he muttered, caught in the act. "I just feel sorry for her, the poor pup. She's got nowhere to go."

"Can we keep her, Dad, pllllleeeeeaaaasssseee," I begged

"Well if it was just up to me," dad started. Then he said, "Gabe, if you really want to keep her, go ask Mom. She is the one you have to convince more than me." He then went back to playing with her.

Later at the breakfast table, as Dad read his paper, I motioned to the screen door and said, "You know, Dad, I think Princess Christina Anna Belle likes you best of all of us!"

Dad grunted and looked at me as though he knew exactly what I was getting at. Meanwhile, Princess had her little black nose pressed against the screen door, just begging him to let her come in.

Dad replied, "Well, she is a very sweet dog."

My mom looked at him sharply, and instructed, "No, no...!"

Dad asked, motioning to the dog, "How could you refuse that little face?"

My mom sighed extra loud, and I knew the deal was all but sealed.

I squealed, "Are we keeping her?"

Without waiting for an answer, I jumped up and opened the back screen door, and the energetic puppy came bounding into the house, landing in my dad's lap where she started licking his face.

Dad looked at me very sternly. "You know you are going to have to feed her and brush her! Her hair is much longer than Frisky's and it needs to be well-kept."

"I'LL DO ANYTHING!" I squealed, so excited, and not believing my own ears.

My mom rolled her eyes, but somehow I knew even though Mom would never admit it that she had fallen for her too, and with that, Princess Christina Anna Belle joined our family. Within a week she was sleeping in my bedroom and bounding all about as though she had lived with us forever.

Frisky seemed to accept her somewhat reluctantly. He made sure she knew that his makeshift pillow-bed was his, and that she wouldn't be sleeping in his bed. It became clear that Princess had more energy than any of us, and so we changed her name from Princess Christina Anna Belle to Friskier.

Soon Frisky, Friskier and I were roaming the fields together, a threesome, seemingly meant to be. I loved dogs...all dogs, that is, except for one: a dog who lived down the road named Killer.

MEET KITTY ¼ AND KITTIER (FLOP)

Our cats couldn't have been more opposite. Kitty was a skinny, gray cat, with a white patch on her chest. She was Bootsie's kitten.

Bootsie had been our black-and-white cat for a time. Bootsie had a habit of disappearing into the fields surrounding our home and returning every couple of months. On one of her returns, she came back missing several toes. We all wondered what she had gotten herself into, and why she didn't want to live with us all the time, but obviously by the way she wandered so often, she didn't. And I never saw her again after that last time with her missing toes.

Before she disappeared for good, Bootsie had had a litter of kittens on the top of the freezer in the garage on one of her trips back to our house. There were six kittens; five were given away, but Kitty stayed.

Kitty stayed close to home, but she had Bootsie's independent streak: she didn't like to be held or cuddled at all, and would run from us if we got too near.

Quite the opposite of Kitty was Kittier. He was the most lovable cat in all of the world. He loved to sit in my lap and nuzzle his face to mine. He also had a deep, throaty MEOW that boomed throughout the house.

We'd inherited Kittier as a kitten from a relative. He was a tiny, black kitten with intense gray eyes, white eyebrows and a white-tipped tail. After he came into our house, he grew to be perhaps the largest cat I have ever seen.

Kittier kept growing until he was several times Kitty's size. He was HUGE. He looked like a giant walking meatloaf with hair. Our two cats would wander around our yard, and often I could see them crossing the gravel road to chase mice in the field across the street. When it was time to feed them, Mom would slide open the kitchen window and stick her electric can opener on the windowsill. The whirr-whirr-whirr sound got their attention. Kitty would perk up and start meowing in her tiny

little voice. Kittier's louder MEOW would echo off the tr
house as he thundered toward the house to eat.

Kitty had to be a fast runner, because if Kittier ever g
there first, she would arrive only to find little food left and a
fat cat that was hard to squeeze around to get to the remaining
food. It was one of these feeding times that would change
Kittier's name.

The cats were heading for the back door for dinner when,
right in mid-stride, Kittier just fell over. He looked dead. I
started yelling for Mom. Kitty just kept speeding toward the
food bowl.

Kittier just lay there still, as dead as a doorknob, then
suddenly his head popped up and he let out one of his huge,
bellowing MEOWS. He shook his head like he had no idea what
had happened, but when he finally got to the food bowl, Kitty
had eaten more than her share.

Soon after, Kittier was sitting on the top of the back of Dad's recliner watching the movement on our tiny black-and-white TV when his eyes rolled back in his head and he went FLOP. The sound of his big body hitting right down onto the carpet echoed through the house. Again he looked totally limp and dead.

After a few more incidents like that, Dad took him to the veterinarian, who diagnosed that Kittier had narcolepsy, a condition that cause those who have it to fall asleep involuntarily at times when they least expect it.

The loud thudding FLOP that reverberated through the house whenever he would fall asleep unexpectedly got poor Kittier his name change. Pretty soon protective pillows started showing up under his favorite places to sun himself or to watch the action going on in the house. People who came over always asked why the piano, the recliner, the dining room hutch and other places had a circle of pillows under them. That was when we decided the name Flop fit him better than Kittier.

Usually you could find Flop sleeping up on my bunk. He favored me, and spent many a night on my bed with me. He was a very lovable, fun cat, but every so often in the middle of the night I would be awakened by the huge thudding FLOP of his body diving off the upper bunk and landing, fortunately, on the pillows on the floor. He would be dead asleep, never knowing he had taken a dive in the middle of the night, when I would lift him back up onto the bunk and position him close to the wall so he wouldn't fall off again.

In addition to the domesticated animals that lived in our home, at any point there would be two or three more animals that I had rescued from the fields. I thought I would grow up to be an animal doctor, like the character from one of my favorite books, Doctor Doolittle.

I rescued salamanders in danger of drying up in window wells they had fallen into, and birds with broken legs and broken wings from some of the careless kids with BB and pellet guns.

Once I had a baby robin named Chirper who had fallen out of the nest and was in danger of drowning in the ditch that ran behind our house.

Chirper lived in my bedroom for longer than a year. My bedroom was like a makeshift animal hospital. Whenever I brought a new animal home I asked Dad first, since he liked animals a lot more than Mom. If it was a questionable animal, namely a reptile, he would give me a Dad look and say, "You better go ask Mom on this one, buddy." Whenever he said that, I figured, why bother?

Luckily, Mom only had one steadfast rule about animals: NO SNAKES! The one time I disobeyed her rule, it backfired on me in a BIG WAY! I had sneaked a five-and-a-half-foot bull snake from the pond across the gravel road into the terrarium in my closet. He would lie in the terrarium with its screened top, coiling around upon himself, and flicking his tongue in and out, when I opened the closet to check on him.

I made the mistake one evening when my parents were out of showing my snake to our babysitter, a teenager with a very odd name: Jilly. Her twin sister, Flower, was our regular babysitter but now had a boyfriend and wasn't as interested in babysitting anymore. Flower was prettier than Jilly and had a better name, which might explain why Jilly was so mean.

You see, I was used to Flower being interested in the stuff in my room. Sometimes we played with my Legos or Tinker Toys, or just listened to my records for hours. Thinking I might get Jilly to like me somehow, I took her to my room and introduced her to Snake and asked her not to say anything to my mom, explaining my mom's severe fear of snakes. She shrugged, sneered and went back downstairs to watch TV and stuff her face with all of our snacks. At some point during that evening, while I watched "Creature Features," Jilly snuck up into my bedroom and let the snake out of the terrarium.

Hours after I had gone to bed, I heard a blood-curdling scream coming from downstairs. My brother and I rushed down to see what was happening. Mom was standing on the kitchen table, shaking from fear and screaming, "GET THAT THING OUT OF THIS HOUSE! WHICH ONE OF YOU BROUGHT THAT CREATURE INTO MY HOUSE?"

The bull snake was wrapped around the table leg, flicking his tongue in and out in Mom's direction. I rushed the snake out to the ditch behind our house and let him go.

When I came in Mom screamed at me at the top of her lungs, "HOW MANY TIMES HAVE I SAID, NO SNAKES? YOU DIRECTLY DISOBEYED ME, AND ALMOST GAVE ME A HEART ATTACK. NO MORE WILD ANIMALS! YOU ARE GROUNDED TO THE YARD FOR A MONTH! Since it was summertime, this was going to be the longest month of my life.

My brother just sat on the stairs, smirking at me and laughing into his armpit. I'd get him back, and somehow I would get Jilly back too.

The next morning Mom and Dad were sitting at the kitchen table arguing about the whole grounding thing. Dad was suggesting that instead of being grounded that I do additional chores around the house. Mom relented and I got off pretty easy.

Dad became my hero. But I never had another snake in the house again.

CHAPTER TWELVE
KILLER

He was this HUGE, snarling, angry dog that lived down on Neptune Drive, and all that any of us neighborhood kids really knew about him was that he was named Killer. The reason we knew that was that from behind a thick, tangled mass of trees and bushes we could hear the gravely, angry voice of his master bellowing at him as he lay near the crudely-painted sign, STAY OFF OF MY PROPERTY!!

Like most things that are forbidden, you get really curious about them. With a group of boys hanging around, you could almost predict the disaster that would follow if they were told there was something they absolutely were not supposed to do or see. There had been rumors for a long, long time about the crazy man who owned Killer. He was supposedly very dangerous and mean.

No one I knew had really ever really seen him close up, but some of the older boys claimed they had caught glimpses of him one terrifying night. Apparently he was about ten feet tall and was really, really mean.

No one had actually ever met him or seen him in daylight. I had heard just about every crazy thing you can imagine about him, but what I did know for sure was that there was a killer dog at the end of his driveway to assure no one ever ventured up there. My dad had told me as far back as I could remember to completely steer clear of the man and his dog. He was some kind of a raving lunatic, and although my dad wasn't really one to go in for believing legends and stories, he said the man at the other end of that driveway was not someone you would want to meet in a dark alley. I wasn't totally sure of why he would say that though, since we didn't have any alleys in our neighborhood. I always hoped to catch a glimpse of the hairy maniac that lived in that house, but I wasn't too interested in having a close encounter with him at all.

The weird man probably didn't get much mail, but the mail he did get would gather around the front of his mailbox and get all puffy and brown from the rain, because the mailman wouldn't dare step even a few inches onto the property to put it in the metal mailbox that had rusted shut for fear that Killer would eat him.

Killer was big and black. He growled, slobbered and snapped at anyone foolish enough to venture too close to his long driveway. I was sure he could eat me in three bites if he was hungry enough. He would lie in wait at the end of the drive, hiding underneath a big bush that camouflaged the driveway.

I watched him from my tree house, and whenever someone would approach, Killer would begin to lick the air as though it were the appetizer for the meal he was about to eat.

When someone walked past Killer, he would lunge as hard as he could, stretching the large silver chain he was attached to. He would attack the air, "AR R R R AR R R ROOOOOF," and whoever was careless enough to pass by so close would bolt off in a full-out run.

One morning as I was heading down the gravel road toward Tunnel Number Three to go fishing for the elusive Carp Monster, I was busy tying new bobbers to my line and accidentally drifted to Killer's side of the road. As I passed his driveway, he lunged out and in his huge, snarling, yellow fangs caught the bottom of my special Sears bell-bottom pants. He began to chew on the pants and was heading toward my leg when Frisky, who was usually very timid around him, ran and jumped on his back, chewing at his neck viciously.

Killer let go of my leg and reached back with his jaws, grabbing Frisky by the throat. He began to shake him like a rag doll. Now Frisky, though half husky and half beagle, had all of the husky's size with the beagle coloring. He wasn't easy to toss about, but Killer made him look like a girl's doll as he shook him with his wild fangs. A bloom of blood spread across Frisky's throat and down Killer's chin.

I panicked, screaming and crying. I took my fishing pole and pulled it apart where the two pieces fit together and clubbed Killer right between the eyes, narrowly missing Frisky with the reel end. Frisky's body had just kind of went limp, and he was whimpering, caught in Killer's jaws, now his throat was all wet with blood. Killer's right eye rolled back like a shark in a feeding frenzy, but his evil left eye locked in on me as if to say I was his next victim. I panicked. He had my best friend in his nasty jaws, and it looked like he was going to break Frisky's neck.

I swung the pole again as hard as I could in a downward motion, like when swinging an axe down to cut a log. The reel caught the huge, nasty dog in the eye on my second whack. Killer let out a huge growling shriek. His mouth suddenly hung slack and Frisky escaped as Killer collapsed to his knees, writhing in pain. Then both of his eyes rolled into the back of his head and closed shut.

I couldn't believe it. I had knocked Killer out cold. Could I go to jail for this? Was Frisky going to die? Frisky just laid down on his side, his lungs filling with air and small whimpering gasps escaping through his lips.

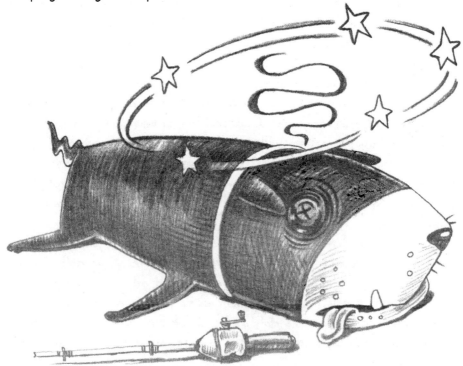

I sobbed. With all that blood I wondered how my dog would ever survive.

I laid down next to Frisky, talking to him, telling him he couldn't die, that I loved him and he needed to get up now. He looked at me kind of helplessly. But I knew we needed to get out of there before Killer woke up again. I had heard stories of what wild dogs do when they are in pain; they kind of just go insane and lash out at anything around them.

Frisky's neck and chest were totally bloody, dark red blood was running down his front legs, and his front leg was torn open to the bone. A huge flap of furry skin hung off the front of his leg, and he was whining really badly. He couldn't walk, and it was all I could do to carry him home. My face was streaked with dust and tears as I headed towards our house. I started screaming when I was about a block from my house.

My dad had just come home from work, and came running out to meet me on the gravel road. He looked at Frisky's leg and told me to get him into his van immediately. He drove his green Volkswagen van as fast as he could to the vet.

His injuries were so serious, Frisky had to spend the night, and I cried myself to sleep. Even Carl was nice to me, seeing how scared and sad I was.

When Frisky came home, it was with instructions to let him lay low for a while so he could heal up. He had stitches, and he licked and licked and licked his wounds. Dad had to carry him up and down the stairs several times a day to go to the bathroom.

Several days later Frisky limped down the stairs and wanted to go out in the backyard. When he did, Friskier stayed close to him the whole time, taking care of him because she was so happy to see him in the backyard moving around a bit.

Soon, Frisky was back to normal and we were roaming the fields together again. From that point on, however, whenever Frisky went down the gravel road toward the fishing holes, he would cross the road about a block before Killer's house, not taking any chances on another encounter.

I followed Frisky's lead.

CHAPTER THIRTEEN

SCARY DEEDEN

In my Big Chief notebook, I had been making tons and tons of notes and drawing pictures about my squirrel, Deeden, but I was having a really hard time making him scary. Yet I really needed to come up with more stories to scare my brother Carl. I knew I would scare him with the insane asylum monster, but a ghost of some kind was needed. It couldn't just be a regular old run-of-the-mill ghost, though. It had to be something truly scary, eerie and terrifying.

Carl was being mean to me one morning, as usual. He chased me into our room and then grabbed Deeden. As I tried to get Deeden back, his ear ripped off. I got really angry and started screaming at him, "YOU HAVE NO RIGHT!" Carl just smirked, punched my arm and left our bedroom.

I sat at my little desk drawing angry pictures, trying to think of a cool way for Deeden's ear to haunt my brother in my stories. But something about a torn squirrel's ear just didn't seem that scary. Then a good idea came to me: what if Deeden's ear was in the top drawer of Carl's dresser drawer, and somehow heard everything Carl said, even if he wasn't in the room? I would work more on that idea to try to make it really scary.

One of the things all the kids in our neighborhood did in the summer was to sit around the fire pit near the community lake under a full moon telling scary ghost stories. It was pitch black down by the lake, and the night sounds were pretty spooky. It was the perfect setting for scaring each other out of our wits.

Some of the older kids, teenagers, would try to tell us things that would make us all leave, because they really just wanted the lake to themselves; but we usually just said, "Yeah, right," to their stories. They weren't very good at telling scary stories, because they never added the details that made them seem like they could happen.

Most of the stories all sounded alike: the scratching on your window at night is the witch's claw; my hand was buried in your backyard and I am coming to get it back. Every story ended up with someone jumping or screaming really loud to startle all of us. I kind of knew when it was coming with most of the guys, because their voices started to get all excited right before they tried to make me jump.

When I told ghost stories I always began them with something that was totally true, or something that sounded totally possible. That way the other guys didn't know what was true and what I was making up. It always worked, and they always wanted me to be the one to tell the next tale. That gave me a brilliant idea for more bunk bed stories.

I stood near the door; it was cracked so I could hear Carl across the hall in Dad's study whispering into the phone. He and his dumb friends Kevin and Greg were planning to meet down at the lake to look for the infamous dead dog later after their parents had gone to bed.

Carl hung up the phone. I ran and jumped up into my upper bunk.

He came lumbering into our room, exhausted. Tossing and turning in the bathtub the last few nights showed on his face now. It was funny to think of him folding his big body into the bathtub; I was so little I could basically stretch out in there, but he had to be so uncomfortable.

As he settled in, I looked down at him and said, "You wanna hear a story?"

"COME ON, GABE! LET UP! I HATE YOUR STUPID STORIES! THEY AREN'T EVEN SCARY, THEY'RE JUST STUPID!"

"Oooh, you are in trouble. You said 'stupid' twice!" Mom had some rules about words we could and couldn't use. "Stupid" was on the forbidden list.

"Shut up, you stupid chicken-dork!"

"Oooh, you are in trouble. You said 'shut up' and 'stupid' again! I'm telling Mom!" "Shut up" was another one of Mom's forbidden words.

"SHUT UP, you STUPID CHICKEN-dork! There, how many is that? Tell Mom and I will give you an Indian rub burn to leave a scar!" Carl whisper-yelled.

Carl was the neighborhood Indian rub burn star. He and his dumb friends would practice that and other torture techniques on each other, and then of course, once they had perfected them, they'd give the real ones to us younger brothers.

I didn't want to push it, because when Carl threatened to give me an Indian rub burn, he usually followed through. "Come on, Carl, I've got a really good story. It's sooooper scary, and it's true, too!"

"Not interested."

"How come?"

"Just not."

"Do my stories scare you?"

"Heck, no!"

"Oooh, you said the h-word, Mom is going to kill you!" Mom
thought that heck was close enough to h-e-double toothpicks that
it was like cussing, so it was another one of her forbidden words.
I could get Carl in SO much trouble if I wanted to, but he'd
make me pay later. It was better to get him to say them where
she could hear him.

"GABE, SHUT UP!" Carl grabbed my arm and started to twist
it hard, one of his fists going forward, one back, the beginning of his
Indian rub burn treatment.

"UNCLE! UNCLE!" I started to yell, loud enough for Mom to hear.

Carl let me up, "I'm serious, squirt, you better shut your mouth or
I'm going to shut it for you!"

"OKAY! OKAY! JEEZ!"

"Oh, look who's talking. I'm going to tell Mom you said 'Jeez.'"
Mom didn't like 'Jeez' either; she thought it was a shortening of
Jesus's name, and we were Catholic. You didn't mess with that one,
because it was one of the BIG TEN.

"Okay! We're even, okay?"

"Even. Now just shut up!"

'Even' was our way of saying we had both gotten caught. It
was like a truce not to tell, though Carl had said about six to my
one J-word. Usually when one of us told Mom anyway she would
say something like, "Nobody likes a tattletale," then yell at the person
who got tattled on.

"Well, first I just want to tell you what my story is about," I taunted.
Carl started to make a move for the door.

"Oh, forget it, you aren't any fun." I was torn between wanting
to scare him so much he would leave and not wanting to sleep in
our room alone. If Carl slept in the bathroom, I wouldn't know
when he was sneaking out, and I planned to follow. I really
wanted to pay him back for all the times he had launched me.

With the quiet in our room, Carl's breathing started to deepen.
He was falling asleep. He was going to miss his rendezvous with
his friends, and I didn't want him to miss it.

In my scariest voice, I began, "One night the tiny gray squirrel
with a torn ear and one of his eyes hanging out came alive and
started tearing through the toy box in the closet, looking and looking
for his other ear... He wanted revenge on the person who had
stolen his ear. His red eyes glowed, the reflection casting an eerie
glow that began to get brighter and brighter."

"GABE, I MEAN IT. KNOCK IT OFF!"

I leaned down into his bunk space, "Are you scared?" Then I thrust
Deeden into his face, holding the small penlight behind his head.

You could have heard my brother's scream all the way down the
street, even as he punched my arm over and over.

CHAPTER FOURTEEN

THE DEAD DOG IN THE LAKE

At about midnight sharks chased me down the river leading into the lake, and then I was face-to-face with the dead dog that was in the lake. Suddenly the dog's eyes opened. His eyes bugged out and then started rolling around, watching me as I tried to swim back up to the surface. Yet something kept pulling me down.

I was startled awake as my bunk bed began to move. I realized I'd fallen into a deep sleep and was dreaming about being underwater, and that it was ridiculous to think sharks could be in the lake. The lake was pretty big, but it was nothing like the ocean.

My favorite part of the lake is a small dock, where I sit for hours and hours and fish. My mom doesn't like me going to the lake alone, and so usually I go down there with a buddy. But sometimes it's just me and my dogs; I like to be alone like that. Dogs are always nice. People aren't.

I heard Carl pull on his jeans and start to tiptoe to the window. I pretended to be asleep. He removed the screen, hopped through the window, pushed the screen back into place and then was gone. I could hear his tennis shoes squishing across the asphalt shingles and then him stepping down onto patio's metal grid work, sliding himself to the ground. His feet pounded down the gravel road, crunching and leaving a sound trail to follow. I wished I had planted the idea of my railroad monster creeping behind the trees, waiting for him, so he would feel some terror as he headed to the lake.

I knew where they'd be meeting, so I could give him a good lead. My dogs were both thumping their tails hard on the ground, thinking it was time for them to get up too. 'Shhhh...' I cautioned. 'You two be good and stay put.'

When I knew my brother must be about a block away, I sneaked out the window, shimmied along the downspout and started running toward the lake. I ran on the dark side of the street, away from the streetlights, ducking around parked cars so no one saw me.

I could see three dark figures up ahead, and I followed along behind them in the shadows. The moon was full and really bright — so bright that it almost looked like daylight out — so I had to be extra careful that none of the neighbors who might call my mom and dad saw me.

I looked up at the stars and couldn't believe how many millions seemed like they were wavering, like water ripples or something, twinkling on and off. I wondered how many aliens must be out there planning a trip to earth.

I was always convinced that if aliens came to earth, they would come to my neighborhood first, on account of all the streets being named after planets. Our neighborhood was called Skyview, and I knew it was because the sky was so big out here at night that it looked like the stars might fall right down on top of you.

I saw my brother and his friends walking around the lake, to where the rowboat was stored in tall weeds. The sound of frogs croaking and crickets by the thousand was deafening. I could smell the algae or moss or whatever it was that made the lake stink like fish poop. Or maybe it was the fish poop that made it smell like fish poop. A weird-sounding bird was making a scary crying sound on the other end of the stream that flowed into the lake, and then he made some splashing sounds. He must have been having a midnight snack.

As usual, I was in my own world, thinking too much and not paying enough attention to what I was doing. As my brother and his friends were taking the easy route around the lake, I was scaling down the sandstone cliff on the other side. The momentum of the hill started to catch up with me as I was looking skyward instead of at my feet, and I began to slip.

They were getting into the rowboat when I suddenly lost
my footing on account of my stupid bad leg. I tripped over
a rock and landed face-first in the lake. I went down deep
in the mossy side, by the cattails, and came up gasping for air.

At the sounds I must have been making they all started
whispering really loud, the sound of their voices carrying over
the water.

"WHO'S THERE?" Kevin whispered like a shout.

I froze.

"WHAT WAS THAT?"

"I DUNNO. GO SEE!"

"YOU GO SEE!"

"YOU!"

"YOU'RE A CHICKEN?"

"Lower your voices, guys. I think old man Patchett's out on
his porch. You guys wanna get caught?" Greg's whispers were
as loud as Kevin and Carl's shouting.

I looked over at Mr. Patchett's tri-level house on the hill
above the lake. It looked like he was sitting on the back
porch. As I stared I could see a tiny red glow come on and
off and on and off and figured it was a cigarette or something.
Suddenly it looked like he stood. His back door opened and I
could see him walk inside. Within a minute he was coming out
the back door and standing there staring at the lake. He had
something big in his hand, and then he started to walk down
across his backyard toward the lake.

If we got caught near the lake at night Carl and I would
be grounded for life. There were only a few things Mom and
Dad totally forbid and the lake was one of them, especially
after dark. I began to panic, thinking Mr. Patchett was going
to catch us.

CHAPTER FIFTEEN

OLD MAN PATCHETT

I was frozen in place, wet and cold, and man it stunk like something had died right where I was. The midnight bird down the canyon kept screaming, and then came a splashing sound. It was starting to feel really spooky, the tension in the air like something really bad was about to happen. I was pretty sure I was the only one who had seen Mr. Patchett leaving his back yard.

"Well, someone's over there," Carl growled.

"Maybe it was just the big carp jumping?" Kevin asked, his voice shaking just a bit.

"Don't be so dumb, Kevin! That carp would have to be huge to make that much noise," my brother snapped.

"Maybe it's a beaver?" Greg joined in.

"A beaver? Come on, Greg, you are such an idiot! There aren't any beavers in this lake!" Carl growled.

"YOU DON'T KNOW THAT!" Greg snapped.

"Then where's the beaver dam, genius?"

"DAM! DAM! DAM!" Kevin shouted, not really cussing. He always thought he was cool if he acted like his older teenage brother.

"SHUT UP! You want old man Patchett to come down here? He's still sore about us stealing his pumpkins last year!" my brother yelped.

"Peters, you shut up. Voices carry over water. You want to get caught?" Greg reminded him.

"What if it's that crazy guy that's running loose you were telling us about, Peters?" Kevin asked.

"Come on, you dork, my chicken kid brother is making all that up. I told you that," Carl whispered, but his voice did carry across the lake just like he was standing next to you.

Dork and chicken, are those the only words my brother knows? I muttered to myself. Then I started to chuckle, thinking about him telling his friends my story. I would have liked to be a fly on the wall to hear his version of it. I was positive he never brought up the fact that it scared him so much he slept in my parent's room.

"Still, what was that noise over there?" Greg whispered.

The bird that was screaming down in the canyon started to holler again. "It was probably just one of those dumb birds with the long legs fishing for carp," Kevin snarled.

Yet I could hear the fear in their voices still.

I was frozen in a crouched position when Greg yelled, "You guys are such wussies!" and started to walk in my direction. I hid in the cattails at the side of the lake, trying desperately to climb up into the taller weeds to hide myself. I splashed down hard again into the muddy water. Greg had a flashlight, and I could see it wildly flashing down, up, down, up, then freeze when he heard the second splash. He waited. I could hear him breathing hard as he crept nearer to where I was trying to be invisible. I knew he was trying to hide the fact that he was really scared.

The light hit me right between the eyes, and he practically screamed, "Peters, you are not going to believe this! It's your idiot kid brother!"

"WHAT?" My big brother sounded furious. "I'm gonna pound him!" The relief in his voice to find out it was not the maniac monster come to eat him was obvious. I could hear him stumbling through the cattails to get over to where we were. I was surprised that Greg had been braver than my annoying brother in investigating what was making the noise.

"Give me your hand!" Greg demanded. I did, and then he yanked me hard out of the lake, twisting my arm behind my back he forced me face-first into the tall weeds.

They scratched my cheek. "OW! LET ME UP, GREG, YOU BIG JERK!

"Shut up!" Greg let go, slapped me across the face when I rose up and then jumped on my back, calling me names as he sneered, "Gabriel Peters is a wuss! What are you doing, spying on us? I ought to pound your ugly face in right here!"

I could hear something coming at us fast through the weeds. The blood in my veins turned to ice. I pictured old man Patchett catching us, or worse, it being some maniac hobo who had wandered off the tracks and was hungry enough to eat a kid.

Suddenly, my brother threw Greg off me, sending him reeling into the weeds. "DON'T TOUCH MY BROTHER, YOU JERK!"

"WHAT?" Both Greg and I said at the same time.

"Greg, you lay another hand on him and I will beat the holy crap out of you!"

Holy crap? I wondered, how can that be religious?

It was so weird that no matter what danger I found myself in, I seem to always get caught on the small things that don't sound right to me....

"Jeez, Peters, I was just messing around. I wasn't going to..." Greg stammered, obviously afraid of my brother like everyone else.

"Yeah, well, don't ever touch him like that again, or I mean it, I will pound you into the ground!" Carl growled.

"Jeez, Peters, calm down, I was just kidding around!" Greg whispered, backing away.

I couldn't believe my ears. Carl was actually sticking up for me.

"What are you doing here, you jerk?" Carl turned his rage back at me.

"I dunno know. I just wanted to see the dead dog, too," I whispered weakly.

"Are we gonna see this dog or not?" Kevin whisper-yelled from the rowboat, which he was paddling slowly in our direction.

My brother grabbed my arm and pulled me along to the side of the lake. "GET IN!" my brother ordered me into the boat.

I climbed in.

"COME ON!" Carl yelled at Greg, who was still sulking.

I guess he didn't want to take any chances that I would go home and tell, or that Mr. Patchett would catch me, getting us all in trouble.

The four of us drifted out to the middle of the lake. The lake was about the size of a professional football field, and when we got to the middle, I figured it to be about thirty or forty feet deep. The three of them shone their flashlights straight down. Water slapped off the dock and the raft, making a loud thwacking sound as small waves moved across the water with the breeze. The rowboat rocked back and forth as the bigger guys stood, and the paddles fell out, drifting away immediately.

"Hey guys, the paddl..." I said.

"Sit there and keep your mouth shut!" Carl barked.

"But the pad..." I tried again.

"Gabe, if you don't want me to throw you in, shut up!" Carl demanded.

I could tell Carl was totally fed up with me, and when he got like that he was dangerous. I didn't want to get punched or thrown in, so I leaned over just enough to see where the beams of their flashlights were shining. No dog to be seen.

"It's down there somewhere! Denny saw it!" Kevin grunted, straining as he leaned over the side of the boat.

"Denny lies about everything! Give me a break," Carl barked.

"I know he saw it, though!" Kevin insisted.

"How do you know?" Greg asked.

Kevin was getting frustrated with Greg and growled, "I dunno! I just do."

"Kevin, you are such an idiot!" Carl snapped. I suppressed a giggle. They were really mean to Kevin who I always thought was a total idiot too, but couldn't get away with talking to him like that.

"Am not!" Kevin whined.

"ARE TOO!" Greg and Carl said together.

"AM NOT!"

"SHUT UP! OLD MAN PATCHETT IS GOING TO HEAR US!" Carl barked.

I spun around and looked back up toward Mr. Patchett's house. Under the full moon, I could see him leaning on the fence at the back of his yard, facing the lake.

"You guys, shhh, Mr. Patchett is watching."

But they didn't hear me. They were too busy arguing and looking for the dead dog that was supposed to be floating about three feet off the bottom, according to Denny, a really weird kid with a blond afro who always had the disgusting habit of spitting on you when he talked. Some kind of anchor weighted the dog down, by holding one leg to the bottom of the lake.

Three lights scanned the entire bottom of the lake, going back and forth. The water was pretty clear on account of the constant flow through the canyons.

It was weird; the stars and moon reflected on the lake like

it was a mirror, but the flashlight beams pierced the water so you could see big fish schooling around under the boat and what looked like miniature lobsters crawling on the floor of the lake thirty feet down. I knew they were actually huge crawdads.

"You guys are losers," I said with my head hanging close to the water now. "There never was a dead dog. Someone would have reported it."

"SOMEONE DID REPORT IT! DENNY DID! TO US!" Kevin scowled.

"Denny's as dumb as you guys are! He's probably somewhere up on the hill watching you idiots fall right into his trap."

"SHUT UP, PETERS!" Kevin barked. "Or is it okay if we tell your brother to shut up now?" he asked, directing his sarcasm at my brother.

My brother took a swing at Kevin, fed up with this whole thing. The momentum of his movement sent both Kevin and Greg reeling into the water, and then the rowboat tipped and sent my brother out the other way. I clung to the bottom of the boat and rode it out, but the splash they had made sent me and the boat spinning toward the end where the water spilled out into Rattlesnake Canyon.

Carl started to swim toward the boat, but his clothes were weighing him down and he wasn't getting close.

Greg and Kevin dog-paddled toward the dock, away from us, when all of a sudden a huge beam of light coming from Mr. Patchett's backyard hit the lake and started to search about.

Greg and Kevin changed directions and started swimming fast toward the other side of the lake near a grove of trees.

I lay down as flat as I could in the rowboat as it rocked back and forth toward the small waterfall. I imagined all of the leeches slithering about in the small pools downstream from the outlet near the dock and the six-foot bull snakes and rattlesnakes lying on the banks of the little river waiting for their next meal to happen down the waterfall. I wondered if, by working together, they could strangle me and pull me under the water to eat me.

"DARN KIDS! ALWAYS CAUSING TROUBLE!" Mr. Patchett snarled. I heard his back gate squeak open and his huge footsteps heading toward the lake, tromping through the weeds and bushes. The bright light shone on my brother's head and followed him as he still struggled to swim to the boat.

Greg and Kevin had made it to a thick grove of cottonwood trees and were hiding.

Mr. Patchett stood on the side of the lake and ordered my brother to swim to him. It was way too far to swim to the other side, and Mr. Patchett could just walk around and beat him anyway, so Carl kept swimming toward him.

Then Mr. Patchett recognized him. "Carl Peters, what in the sam hill are you doing out in the lake at this time of night?"

My brother stammered, "Uh, nothing Mr. Patchett, just thought I'd take a swim, that's all."

"Hmmm, right. You alone? Someone else in that rowboat?"

The boat was drifting to the side. It would be easy enough for Mr. Patchett to figure out who was in it. Carl said, "Uh, it's just me and my brother. He's out there."

"Your momma know you're down here?"

"Uh."

"Don't bother lying to me. I know good and well there is no way your momma would let you boys swim in the lake at midnight.

Shoot, it's more like one o'clock in the morning!"

"Please, Mr. Patchett, don't tell my mom. I'll get grounded for a year."

"GOOD! Then maybe you thieving fiends will stay offa my property."

"Please?" My brother sounded like a little kid pleading with Mr. Patchett.

"Sure sounded like there were more voices down here from where I sat. You sure you don't wanna tell me about the other boys?"

Kevin and Greg lay as still as they could in the cottonwood trees. "He better not rat us out, that's all I can say," Greg whispered.

"Oh, yeah, tough guy, what would you do about it? Peters could whip you with one arm tied behind his back," Kevin whispered hoarsely.

"YOU, TOO!" Greg snorted back.

"Shhh! You wanna get caught too?" Kevin got as low as he could in the thick brush.

The side of the lake Mr. Patchett stood on had a slippery, muddy embankment. He pulled my brother out with one arm. "Sit there!" he commanded and started walking toward the dock, where the rowboat was now drifting.

The dock had a long rope wound on a ring. Mr. Patchett unraveled it and threw it out to me, then towed me in.

When I was on the dock Mr. Patchett said, "Carl, come over here." The three of us now stood on the dock. I could see in the moonlight that Mr. Patchett was barely taller than my brother. "Now, do you two want to tell me what is going on here?"

I stood there dead silent, and Carl began to offer some lie about a dare from one of the older kids and that we meant no harm. I knew he was lying because there was no way anyone was going to say anything about the dead dog to an adult. Even a kid could figure out that if there really was a dead dog tied to the bottom of the lake, then that meant someone had put it there. Someone mean and crazy enough to do that was someone no one wanted to mess with. For a moment, the thought that it had been Mr. Patchett who put the dog there occurred to me, sending a shiver up my spine. What might he do to us?

"FOLLOW ME!" Mr. Patchett said in a sort of nighttime shout-whisper. We did, and then the three of us were standing on his back porch. He went inside, and I looked out at the lake. Greg and Kevin were sneaking down the path back to their houses. They were probably sleeping in the tent in Kevin's backyard so his parents would never know they were out. They were lucky!

Mr. Patchett came back out onto the back porch with a phone to his ear. Carl and I looked at each other with horror.

"Yes, I'm sorry to wake you up so late, but I thought you should know... Yes, I'll keep them here. See you in five." I went totally cold.

"Boys, you're father is on his way."

Carl looked at me with what looked like real terror in his eyes. You never knew how Dad was going to react to something like this. Sometimes the things you would think would make Dad the maddest didn't, and sometimes things that didn't seem like that big of a deal really made him boil.

I wondered why Mr. Patchett couldn't have just let us go home on our own, just let it be our secret.

We were all standing out on Mr. Patchett's back porch waiting. No one was talking. It was the longest ten minutes of my life, just staring at the lake, doing everything possible not to make eye contact with Mr. Patchett or my brother.

Mr. Patchett flipped open his silver lighter and lit another cigarette. A cloud of smoke went up and then disappeared up in the air. I didn't like the way it smelled at all. I remember Mom talking about how Mr. Patchett's wife had died or something from smoking, and wondered how he could still do it.

I thought I would burst out crying at any moment, thinking about the trouble I was going to get in, so I just stared at the same spot imagining that poor dog floating out there in the lake getting eaten away by all kinds of fish and crawdads and other creepy stuff down near the bottom. I imagined his body disintegrating into the lake bottom. There would be no sign that

he had lived, no one to remember him, no place to mark his grave.
I was sad for the dog and wondered why someone would be
that mean.

I was so nervous about Dad coming. Would he tell Mom?
Would it just be between us guys? I had no idea how he was
going to react. Usually if we got into some trouble he was okay
about it, but being down at the lake was another matter. The
danger there might make my dad hit the ceiling.

I heard footsteps coming around the house. Mr. Patchett
went out to meet him, and then my dad and Mr. Patchett shook
hands, and Mr. Patchett clapped dad on the back like they were
good buddies. They both stood by the gate talking in low murmurs
while my brother and I waited there scared to death of what
was coming next.

I caught little snatches of the conversation: "Well, since
that girl drowned..." "Their mother would be out of her mind if
she knew." "Uh huh..." and "Not sure telling her is a good idea..."

Several times they both chuckled lowly about something.
I wasn't sure whether that should make me mad or relieved
that somehow they found something funny about this whole thing.

That dumb bird was still making all kinds of noise down in
the canyon. Now it sounded like he was laughing at us too.
I had noticed when he screamed that it kind of sounded like he
was talking; I figured out that he was saying, "Iiiiiseeeeeyouuuuuu."
I wanted to ring his neck.

"Come on boys, let's go home," Dad called out to Carl and me
in a voice that I couldn't tell if it was angry or not.
"Fred, we'll have to have another poker night soon. Thank you
for your call. I assure you my boys won't be any more trouble for
you, least-wise not at midnight."

Mr. Patchett looked at Carl and me as he said, "Oh, and
speaking of midnight, by the way, boys, did you know there is a
legend about that lake? They say that about a hundred years
ago an old Indian who was tossed in the lake by some roughriders
drowned in there and has haunted it ever since."

The bird screamed, "Iiiiiseeeeeyouuuuuu".

"He's waiting for someone to fall in the lake at midnight to take his place right after he drags them to the bottom and scalps them. But he only surfaces on nights like this when there is a full moon. You boys are lucky he didn't get you, especially you, Carl, since you went in the drink near the middle. I have to say, though, it isn't really a legend, since I have seen him down there from my porch myself."

Fear rushed through me; I had been in the water too tonight, twice.

"FRED, STOP!" Dad yelled. "I HAVE NEVER TOLD MY BOYS THAT STORY! I DIDN'T WANT THEM TO KNOW ABOUT IT UNTIL THEY WERE OLD ENOUGH TO HANDLE IT!"

Dad looked shocked. I huddled as close to Dad as I could without being too obvious.

"So sorry, Peters," Mr. Patchett said. "I've always had such a big mouth..."

Dad shook his head, then turned to us and said, "You boys need to get to bed. Your mother slept through the phone ringing and me getting dressed and sneaking out, but she's bound to notice I'm gone at some point and come looking. If she sees you both are gone too, there will be hell to pay!"

I hadn't ever heard my dad say that word before. He must have really been mad.

On the way home, Dad suggested that we sleep out in our backyard tent, which we pitched on the first day of summer every year. "Your mom won't be any wiser that way while I figure out what I am going to say and what I won't. By the way, when you get in your sleeping bags, stay put the rest of the night: no wandering around, or you'll both really be in big trouble!"

We rode the rest of the way home in silence. It was weird; for some reason, Dad had this small smile on his face, like he was proud of us instead of being too mad. I wondered if he was thinking of the trouble he and my uncles got in to when he was my age. Sometimes when we did stuff Dad kind of bragged about it to his friends and to my uncles later, like we had been doing what we were supposed to.

When we got home Dad walked us around to the backyard. "It's late, boys. Go to sleep, and we will talk about this in the morning."

"Dad, what's our punishment?" I asked. Carl flashed me a dirty look, as though without me mentioning it wouldn't have occurred to Dad to punish us.

"Hmm, well, we will talk in the morning. I'll have to think on this..."

Carl grimaced at what Dad said.

As Dad headed for the house, he called back in a spooky whisper, "And watch out for crazy dead Indians. It is a full moon after all and now that you know... he'll know you know."

I jumped into my sleeping bag and got as deep in as I could. I knew Carl and I both hoped Dad would decide on our punishment alone, because Mom was a bit stricter about things like this that involved danger, like the railroad tracks and the lake.

The next morning Carl and I piled into the kitchen. Mom was standing at the stove humming. The smell of bacon filled the whole house. My mouth started to water.

"Gabe, you look tired. Didn't you sleep well?"

Carl rubbed his eyes, and Mom turned her eyes on him.

"Carl, you too. You boys look like you didn't sleep a wink last night!"

I wondered if Dad had told her, and she was fishing for information. My mom considered it worst thing if you lied. "I'm okay..." I sputtered.

Carl said, "You know, the first night in the tent...it's just different, that's all..."

"Hmmm," Mom said.

I wondered what she knew.

Dad came down the stairs smiling. "Morning, boys!"

"Morning, Dad!" we said in chorus, both a bit ashamed.
Dad walked over and kissed Mom's cheek, "Morning, honey."
"Morning."
"That smells mighty fine, doesn't it, boys?"
"Mmm hmmm," we both answered.
"Say boys, can I see you in the backyard for a moment?
I need to talk to you about some chores I need you to do today."
    We both stood, petrified, and followed behind Dad. When
we got outside of Mom's earshot, Dad said, "Do you boys know
how dangerous the lake can be?"
    We both just nodded in reply.
    "Do you know what would happen if you boys pulled that
stunt again?"
    We both stood there stock-still.
    "Here's the deal. I need a lot of help around here. I figure
about two days worth for both of you. Usually I would pay you
for it, but let's consider this your punishment this time. And, I'm
not going to tell your mother about this either; it's just between
us, okay?"
    I couldn't believe my ears. Mom would have grounded us for
a month, maybe the whole summer, if she had taken the phone
call from Mr. Patchett! This was the second time Dad had come
to my rescue when it came to getting grounded.
    We both nodded and spent the next two days cleaning the
basement, the garage, the shed, the garden, our rooms, the kitchen,
the bathrooms, and crawlspace. We even painted the downstairs
bathroom. By the end of the two days I wondered if it might
have been worth it to get grounded.

CHAPTER SIXTEEN
MUSIC MAN

While we were cleaning out the crawlspace, I found a lot of neat stuff that I didn't even know was down there... stuff Mom and Dad had been carrying around since they were kids.

In the back of the crawlspace, covered with spider webs, spider eggs, and dust galore, was a really cool old guitar. I blew it off and strummed it. My brother growled, "GET BACK TO WORK!"

"Put a sock in it!" I yelled, crawling out of the crawlspace to set the guitar out in the basement. I turned back to fit the latch onto the small door leading into the crawlspace from the house.

My brother started to bang on the door as hard as he could. "LET ME OUT OF HERE, GABE! I AM GOING TO POUND YOU!"

When he stopped trying to open the door, I released the latch so he could open it if he wanted to, but he didn't know that.

Dad came bounding the stairs. "What is all that racket?"

"I dunno. Carl is having a cow about something, Dad."

Dad smiled. He had done the same kind of stuff to his older brother, my Uncle Morris. "Hey, my old guitar! Man, I haven't played that thing since I was dating your mom. I used it to sing ballads of my love to her. Won her heart with that guitar, I did." Dad looked like he was far away.

"Gross, Dad, I don't want to hear about it," I said.

He smiled and grabbed the guitar from my hands and started to strum it, coughing from the dust that came off of it. He started to sing, "I love the way your sparkling earrings... against your skinnnn so brownnnn..."

"GROSS ME OUT, DAD!"

Dad winked. "Works like a charm when you want to win a girl over buddy. Worked for me, go ask your Mom..."

Carl pushed up against the door and fell into the room. "HEY, WHAT GIVES? HE LOCKS ME IN THE CRAWLSPACE AND NO ONE DOES ANYTHING TO HELP ME!"

"Stop being so melodramatic Carl!" Dad, said and then he continued singing.

"I wanna sleep..." he stopped abruptly. "Oh, never mind. Wow, it's been a long time."

"You sound good, Dad. I didn't even know you knew how to

play the guitar," I said.

"You want this old thing, Gabe?" Dad asked.

"NOT FAIR!" My dumb brother yelled. "What about me?"

"Since when are you interested in the guitar, or any music, for that matter?" my dad asked.

"Since when is that squirt interested?" Carl pouted back.

"Gabe's always listening to his radio. Don't fight over it, boys. You can share."

"But it's mine, right, Dad?" I asked.

"Sure, buddy, it's all yours."

I gave Carl a dirty look.

Carl sulked and headed back into the crawlspace. "COME ON, CHICKEN-LOSER, LET'S GET THIS JOB FINISHED!"

"Carl, don't call your brother a chicken or a loser," Dad winked at me.

Carl stormed back into the crawlspace.

After we finished with all of the chores Dad wanted help with, I polished the guitar with a rag and some wood polish and took it to my room. I turned my transistor radio on, jumped up onto my bunk with my guitar and tried to play along with some of the songs on my favorite station K I M N. I thought I sounded pretty good. The dogs just looked at me curiously.

I kept strumming and singing when all of a sudden Flop fell off the top bunk onto a small pile of pillows, dead asleep. Though I had seen it so many times, it made me laugh every time. "I'm that bad, huh, Flopster?"

Flop woke up a few minutes later and meowed his big gruff MEOW, then jumped up on the lower bunk and gave himself a bath.

The next morning I walked down toward my friend Eddie's house to see if he wanted to go fishing.

I was passing Mr. Patchett's and noticed him sitting on his front porch drinking a cup of coffee and reading the morning newspaper. He looked up at me and started patting his mouth, making a singsong Indian song and laughing. Then he grabbed his necktie and held it over his head, like he was being hung, rolled his eyes in the back of his head and stuck his tongue out.

"Very funny, Mr. Patchett," I said under my breath and walked on.

There was a big garage sale sign at the end of a long gravel

driveway near Eddie's house that caught my eye. I started up
the driveway. The folks that lived up in that house were from
somewhere far away. They talked funny, and I didn't know much
about them except that they had a son and a daughter who
were old enough to leave home.

When I got to the top of that long driveway I couldn't believe
my eyes. The whole garage and flat part of the driveway were
filled with so many treasures, things no one in their right mind
would want to get rid of. There were bicycles, hoses, tools, books
and tons of old-fashioned toys. I overheard the lady telling
another neighbor that they were going to move to a city to be
close to their grown-up daughter who used to babysit me when
I was real little and would let Carl and me eat cereal and ice
cream for dinner.

As my eyes and hands swept over the stuff they called junk,
I was stopped cold. On a big coffee table there was a very cool

phonograph turntable and a huge box of 45 records. Each had a
piece of tape with a price written on it. The phonograph was $5.00,
and the records were $3.00 for the whole bunch, what a bargain!!
There must have been ten thousand records in that box, and I
wanted them so badly. I thought of how many songs I could
learn with my new guitar if I had a record collection like that.

In my Snoopy piggy bank at home, I had been saving my
allowance and working as many odd jobs as I could to earn
back my Hot Wheels money after the underwear incident. I
knew, because I counted it so often, that I had exactly $3.75.
I needed another $4.25 to buy the records and phonograph.

The old man who lived there moved over next to me. 'Chuu like
museek?' he asked in his thick accent. It was kind of hard to
understand him.

"Yeah, I do!' I liked the way he said 'music.'

'That was my boy'z. He doesn't want no more. Ach, I don't
unnerstand him, in the old country we use everyting, long time.'
He rolled his eyes for some reason. 'Chuu want that?'

"Yeah, but I don't have enough money.'

'Chuu mow my grass this summer, until we move, it's yours.'

I hadn't mowed a whole lawn before. Dad let me mow the
backyard with him sometimes, but not alone. 'I'd have to ask my
mom and dad.'

'Chuu like the drum?' He motioned to the back of the garage
and nodded for me to follow him. He pulled a yellowed sheet off
of an entire shiny silver drum set.

'Uh, I've never played drums before.'

'Chuu like to learn, eh?'

I thought of my piano lessons which Mom made me go to, which
I hated for too many reasons to list, but mostly because my piano
teacher, Mrs. Stolz, spit when she talked and usually on my cheek.
I'd much rather play the drums. I wondered if the little old man
was offering to give me drum lessons. "You play these?'

He laughed. 'Ach, no. These my sons too. Chu want?'

"WHAT?'

'My son in hippy commune out in California. He no longer
wants any of this things. He's crazy!'

I thought about his son. I remembered him driving fast up and down our dirt roads in a hopped-up Camaro, which all of us boys thought was the coolest car in the world. I looked around for the Camaro, figuring if I stayed longer the old man might offer it to me, too.

"Chuu mow my grass and help me with boxes and other moving things, and then the drums, phonograph and records can all be yours. Chuu nice boy, I know, lots of help. I just don't need it around here no more."

My stomach jumped. I could hardly believe my ears. Dad had been talking about moving his office down to the basement and letting my brother and me have our own bedrooms. The drum set would fit in there, and I would have my very own music in my very own room. I couldn't believe he would let me have all this stuff just for doing some work around his place.

"I'll be right back, I have to go ask my mom and dad." I yelled as I ran as fast as my legs would carry me down his driveway, which wasn't too fast on account of my bum leg. I needed to get home and back in record time before the little old man offered the same deal to another kid.

I ran into the house totally out of breath, up the stairs to Dad's office.

"DAD! DAD!"

Dad was nowhere to be found.

"MOM! MOM!"

I ran back down the stairs to the kitchen.

"Down here, Gabe!" I headed down into the basement. Mom was downstairs sewing a dress on her sewing machine. I shuddered when I saw this really spooky-looking half-body dummy with no head that Mom put her dresses on when she was sewing them from a pattern.

"MOM! MOM!" I was breathing really hard.

Mom came bolting up the stairs, meeting me half-way. I turned and we both ended up in the family room, Mom following me as I tried to catch my breath.

"GABRIEL, WHAT HAPPENED?"

Mom's face was as white as a sheet. I had come in from the fields so many times cut up and bruised that she must have thought I had gotten hurt again.

"YouknowthosepeoplethatliveupontheMilkyWayHill?Hetoldme IcouldhavehisdrumsandhisrecordplayerandhisrecordsifImowed hislawnandIreallyreallywantto."

"Calm down Gabe, I can't understand you. Just slow down and tell me."

Dad came walking in from the garden. "What's all the ruckus?"

I began again. "That man that talks funny up on Milky Way Hill told me that if I could mow his lawn this summer he would give me a drum set and record player and a billion records. Can I, please? Can I?"

Dad looked at Mom.

Mom said, "Mow his lawn? That's a dangerous job, Gabe. We agreed to wait until you were older to mow our lawn, so..."

"BUT MOM!" I practically yelled at her.

"And a drum set? Come on, Gabe, they are so loud." Mom looked over at Dad.

"BUT MOM!"

"I always wanted to be a drummer. They got all the groovy chicks," Dad said with a wide smile.

Mom swatted Dad with the material in her hand. "Oh, please."

He kept smiling at her. "Drums are fun and great for coordination."

"But, can he mow their whole lawn? What if..."

"Well, he doesn't just want me to do it once," I interrupted, "but for the whole summer, and I can do it, I swear!"

"Hmm, well, why don't I go up there with you and talk to Mr. Povich about it," Dad volunteered.

"LETS GOOOOO, DAD, COME ON!"

Mom started nodding her head, looking at Dad. He looked at Mom, shrugged and then we were off to go make a deal with Mr. Povich.

CHAPTER SEVENTEEN

THE LITTLE DRUMMER BOY

Mr. Povich and Dad talked for a while while I drooled over the record collection. I thumbed through the albums: Led Zeppelin, Rolling Stones, The Who and a ton of other rock-and-roll albums. Then I looked at the tables full of stuff that had been in the Povich's house and now was going to be in a hundred houses. All kinds of ladies were looking through clothes and junk. I looked up, and now Dad and Mr. Povich were in the back of the garage looking at tools and stuff. I walked back, afraid to say too much, but desperately wanting to know what they decided.

"Well, I'll take all of these over here." Dad motioned to a stack of hoes, rakes and other lawn stuff. "And this stuff, too." He pointed at the workbench, where he had made a pile of stuff he already had at home. "I'll walk home and bring back my van. You show Gabe the ropes."

My stomach leaped. Was Dad saying what I thought he was?

Mr. Povich and Dad shook hands. Dad grinned at me and shrugged, then started down the driveway.

"Vell, Gabriel, let me chow you chust how my mower wurks."

I felt so grown up. I couldn't believe my ears. I followed Mr. Povich around back to his shed. He pulled the mower out and showed me how to check the oil and gas and how to empty the bag. He then motioned for me to push the mower down to the edge of the back lawn.

When I got there, I pulled and pulled the cord trying to start it, hoping Mr. Povich wouldn't change his mind, thinking I was just some dumb kid.

"Oops, I forget to tell. Chuu have to bull ze choke out. My vault."

I pulled a lever out and then pulled again. It started on the second pull, vibrating my arms as I began to push it through the tall grass. I made several passes up and down as Mr. Povich stood nodding at me.

He then yelled over the mower, "Overlap, one veel in the otherz path!"

I saw behind me the small strip of grass I had left behind. I pulled the mower backwards to cut the thin swath. Mr. Povich gave me the thumbs up, and looked around to the driveway, making a sign across his throat to kill the engine. Dad was pulling up the driveway.

"Come, Gabriel, chuu help your vather."

We walked around to where Dad was smiling from ear to ear. He had seen me pushing the mower, the handle just even with my eyes.

"Gabe, you look like an old pro with that thing."

He flipped a pair of safety goggles at me. "Mom agreed under one condition: that you wear these, so make sure you do."

I nodded, putting them on over my glasses and then pushed them up onto my forehead.

"Come on buddy, let's load those drums in here," Dad told me.

"WHAT? ALREADY? But I haven't done my jobs yet."

"Mr. Povich needs them out of his garage, and he says he trusts you."

Mr. Povich nodded and carried one of the drums out of the garage.

A little boy was begging his dad for a big bag of Legos that he wanted really bad. "Dad, can I, please? Can I? Can I?"

His dad, who seemed totally occupied with an old radio built in this big cabinet, looked up and said, "I dunno. Go ask Mom." I smiled, thinking that all dads must say that a million times a day.

We loaded the drums, phonograph, records and a ton of garden tools into Dad's Volkswagen van. When we were done, Mrs. Povich met us with a tray of homemade cookies and lemonade. We sat in the shade under a crabapple tree listening to Mr. Povich talk about his son Lenny who had played those drums and listened to the records by the hour. Mr. Povich's eyes looked sad and got all wet when he talked about him. I felt sad that he missed him so much.

When the cookies were gone and the lemonade drunk, Mr. Povich looked like he was going to take a nap right there in his chair. Dad said, "Okay, son, you finish mowing the lawn and any other chores Mr. Povich needs you to do, then come home and we'll put this stuff in your new room."

"WHAT? MY NEW ROOM?"

"Well, I have been wanting to move my desk downstairs for a while, and Mom's other condition about you having drums is that you have a door to close when you practice, so today is moving day! Carl wants my study. Do you mind staying in your current room?"

"MIND? I LOVE MY ROOM!" Dad looked at me like I had lost my marbles. I was so excited I could hardly stand it. I hugged Dad so tight his face turned red and so did mine. I watched his van go down the driveway, and thought I was the luckiest kid in the world to have such a great dad.

As I mowed the Povich's backyard, I looked over at Mr. Povich sleeping under the tree as people carted away parts of his life, and wondered if his son knew he too had a great dad.

When I got home Dad already had moved most of his office

stuff to the basement. 'I need help with the desk and the
chairs and the file drawers,' he told me.

We tried to lug the heavy stuff down the two small flights of
stairs, with Dad taking the downhill, heavy end, but he ended up
having to ask our neighbor Mr. Morris to help him move the heavy
desk. They stood around talking while I waited impatiently to
start moving Carl's stuff out of our shared room and into his
new room.

I felt really excited about finally having my very own room
with a door that I could shut Carl out with. Besides, I had the
best room: the roof was right under my window, allowing me to
sneak out when I needed to meet my friends for a nighttime
rendezvous! Usually all we did was sneak out and meet in the
backyard tent, which we were allowed to sleep in every night
if we wanted to anyway. I knew Dad knew about the escape
route, and acted like he didn't.

I decided I was going to keep the bunk beds in my room for
sleepovers. And now, with Carl no longer sleeping in the lower
bunk, I could make cool forts by draping big covers and sheets
from the upper bunk to the floor.

Finally Mr. Morris left and Dad, Carl, and I spent the
afternoon moving stuff across the hall and filling boxes full of
stuff neither me nor Carl used anymore for the crawlspace.

By the time it got dark I had my very own room. Mom said
we could pick out some wallpaper from these cool, huge books
that she had gotten at the paint store in town. She also told
us she would take us to Musicland and we could each pick out
a few posters, which would make our rooms really ours. I felt
really grown up all of a sudden, but inside I felt a little scared,
too. My room got awfully dark at night, and being in there
alone was going to take some getting used to.

It was a good thing Carl had been spending as much time
as he had sleeping in the bathtub lately.

Over the next several weeks, I did so many chores for Mr.
and Mrs. Povich that I was really tired when my head hit the
pillow. Just for fun, Carl slept in the lower bunk a few times.
Neither one of us would ever admit it out loud, but we kind of

missed each other, weird as it sounds. Besides, he could have launched me, and I would have slept right through it I was so exhausted from working so hard.

I played the drums until my wrists were sore. I strummed the guitar and listened to record after record, choosing my favorites, which tended toward the loud rock- and-roll style.

Mr. Povich sold his house pretty quickly, so I only had to mow his lawn six times. I did help him a lot the last week before they moved as he was cleaning out his garage and basement, getting ready to move. I liked him, and it made me wish that I had gotten to know Mr. Povich a long time ago.

Every time we would stop to rest, we would eat homemade cookies and drink sweet tea or lemonade and he would tell me the coolest stories, not like other old people stories my grandpa tells over and over about all the medical conditions every single one of his friends has, but really cool stories about wars and stuff. Mr. Povich had been a soldier in a bunch of real bloody battles and didn't mind telling all the cool stuff that most adults think kids shouldn't hear. He showed me a real bad scar on his shoulder, and when I told him I was sad for him, he said, 'Ach, this I get saving lady and baby from evil men. I am proud of these scar.'

I hauled box after box of cool stuff home that Mr. Povich just gave me. Mom wasn't too pleased about all of it stacking up in the living room, so I moved most of it to the crawlspace. I thought that sometime when I had a lot of time I could go through the boxes.

But one thing led to another, and soon I forgot about the boxes.

I wouldn't forget Mr. Povich. He had turned me on to some of my lifelong greatest loves: music and adventure stories.

SECRET DETECTIVE BROTHERHOOD

There were six of us younger brothers living out in Skyview. All of us constantly complained about how mean our older brothers were and planned how we might get back at them.

Eddie was in fifth grade but really small for his age, and then there were me, Andy, Craig, Tony, Butch and Tyler, who were all in fourth grade. Each of us had a brother in the older group that my brother hung around with.

We hung around together a lot, and usually met in the tree house across the street from my house or in one of the dirt forts in the wheat field just west of our neighborhood. We were forming a club, but it was kind of hard with Andy gone, and now Eddie had to go to Florida to visit his grandma. He was going to be gone a whole month, which I thought was horrible since I considered Eddie my second best friend in the whole world, right after Andy. I would never tell the other guys that, though.

As we met secretly up in the tree house we made a plan to spy on our older brothers and keep records of all of the things they did that we could get them in trouble for.

I had made an ID card for each of us to stick in our wallets. Here was mine:

> The secret detective brotherhood
> We solve crimes big and small
> This card belongs to Gabriel Peters

We also traded our hot rod car stickers and baseball trading cards with each other. Craig Turner had an entire collection of Odd Rod stickers and Mad magazines that he brought up in a paper bag to share with us. I had a ton of Archie comic books I showed the guys; I was secretly in love with Veronica and Betty. Trouble was, I was much more like Jughead than Reggie or even Archie, and girls never looked at me the way Veronica and Betty looked at Archie and Reggie.

We all started talking about what kind of names we should have to be secret detectives.

"I'll be Alfred, you know like Alfred E. Neuman!" Craig said excitedly

"More like Alfred the butler," Brad thumped Craig's shoulder.

"Yeah right, that guy's a weenie!" Craig said

"What? Batman's butler's not a weenie? No way dude, he's cool!" Butch complained.

"You're a weenie Butch! Besides Butch is already a nickname, you can't have another one."

"I can too!" Butch jumped on Brad and started wrestling him.

"Guys, we're like a hundred feet off the ground, knock it off!" I said. Those guys are so dumb sometimes.

"Butch, what is your real name?"

"Not telling you geeks, no way!"

"Oh come on, it can't be that bad?"

"No way!"

"I know what it is..." Brad sneered. Brad had been acting like a jerk lately, kind of like his big brother Trey, who was always a jerk.

We went on talking about nicknames for awhile and then got bored with it and decided to stick with our own names.

As we sat in the tree house goofing around, I pulled out my binoculars and started looking all around the neighborhood. Right down by the dirt track, where we all jumped the small hills on our bikes, were two of our brothers. "Hey geeks, there's my brother with Kevin."

"I hate Kevin!" Tyler said about his own brother.

"Hate?" I asked.

"H-A-T-E!" Tyler spelled out. "I totally hate him. That idiot got me in so much trouble this morning, it's a wonder I ain't grounded all summer!"

"For what?" Craig asked.

"I ain't telling!" Tyler snarled back, sounding much like his brother Kevin.

"What are they doing?" I mumbled to myself as I held the binoculars to my eyes.

"HERE, LET ME SEE THOSE!"

Tyler tried to grab the binoculars out of my hands.

"Hang on, man! What's your deal today, Tyler? You are being such a jerk!"

I watched Carl and Kevin walking toward the railroad tracks. "Come on, let's go spy on them and see what they are up to!"

"BOOO-RING!" Tyler complained.

"Why don't you go home then, Tyler, you're being a real turd!" I sneered.

"Why don't you go home, jerko?" Tyler growled.

I started ignoring him. When he got like that he was no fun to be around.

"I don't care if you guys don't want to spy on them. I'm going." I started to climb out of the tree.

"Peters, put your dogs in the house! They'll give us away," Craig grunted.

"Hey Gabe, can you spend the night tonight?" Butch yelled to me when I got down to the ground.

"I dunno. I'll go ask Mom!"

I didn't really want to spend the night at Butch's house. His mom always made really weird dinners. I could never think of a nice way to tell her I didn't want seconds, and she always plopped more on my plate. The cool thing about his house though was that his dad worked for some company that distributes candy and gum, so their garage always is full of candy. It even smells like a Halloween bag inside their house, but after a while, it kind of gives me a headache.

Tyler now walked towards his house, obviously not going with us to spy. He called back, looking over his shoulder, "Hey, if you guys think of something a little more interesting to do, give me a call."

"Don't call us, we'll call you!" Craig said.

We all busted out laughing and headed into the field.

We followed the older brothers down past the lake, and then down to Tunnel Number One where they met up with Greg. Then they just stood around talking. We got bored, and started walking down the tracks singing, "One Hundred Bottles of Beer on the Wall!"

"Remember that time we smashed all those pennies and Tyler got hit by one of 'em when the train went by?" I asked.

"Oh, man, he cried like a baby!" Craig laughed.

"Well, dang, that would hurt. Could have killed him if it hit his head," Butch said kindly.

"He sure made a big production out of it!" Craig sneered.

Butch said "Well, he still has a big scar on his leg from it!"

I didn't like the fact that Craig wanted to make fun of Tyler when he wasn't there. I knew what it felt like to be made fun of, and even though Tyler was acting so dumb, he still was one of my best friends.

Butch said, "Yeah, that ain't cool to make fun of Tyler."

Tony came running over from one of the tunnels. "Hey, what's up guys?" he said a little out of breath.

"Just hanging out!" I said "Wanna come?"

Tony nodded and started kicking rocks down the tracks.

Craig got totally quiet. We walked along the railroad track pitching rocks at fence posts and kicking at the spikes, hoping one might be loose to add to our collection. We already had about twenty railroad spikes hammered into our tree house tree. It took all of us to bang them in with Dad's sledgehammer, but they worked pretty cool as hand and footholds on the tree.

We got a couple miles down the tracks when Craig pointed at something big lying near the track ahead. "LOOK AT THAT, DUDES!"

We ran over to the huge, brown, bloated thing lying beside the tracks. It was a dead raccoon. Craig prodded it with a stick.

"Pee-eww, man, that stinks!" Butch held his nose.

We got closer to it. It was missing a good part of its face, so we figured the train had gotten it. We couldn't figure out why it was so huge; though; it was all blown up like a balloon. You could barely tell it was a raccoon, except for its stripes.

"I'll give you a buck if you eat its ear," Tony taunted Craig who was still sulking.

"SHUT UP, TONY!" Craig barked.

"Chicken?"

"You eat it!" Craig taunted Tony.

"Uh, no." Tony backed away from it. He looked scared, like we were going to pressure him into actually eating it.

I had seen big raccoons before, but this one was as round as a pig. Craig nudged it with his foot, and it made a hollow balloon sound. He then put his boot on it, and pushed down hard. It made a funny loud farting noise, like my grandpa. We laughed so hard I almost peed my pants.

Butch pushed on its stomach again, and it farttttteeeeeedddd out air. Suddenly the hot air around us was suffocating. The stench surrounded us like a clinging cloud we couldn't get away from. It was so strong that all at once Craig, Butch and I threw up. Tony, who had backed way away, was laughing really hard at us. It was so gross.

We threw a bunch of rocks at it. The rocks catapulted off wildly since its stomach was still blown up like a huge, hairy balloon. After a while we got bored with it, and walked along talking about dead things all the way home.

I threw a rock at a barn in the field. "You guys are so retarded. Come on, let's do something else."

When I got home I called Tyler to tell him all about the raccoon. Then I asked him why he had been acting so weird. He mumbled something about wishing his dad would move out.

I felt really bad for Tyler. His dad sometimes hit him and his brothers. Tyler even told me one time that his dad hit his mom.

I wished Tyler could come live with my family. My dad would never hit him.

Tyler and I went back to see the raccoon the next day. It was so freaky: something was moving under its skin, and it was covered with black flies. I threw a rock at it, and about ten zillion flies jumped off and then leaped right back on it. It was SO gross, but SO cool.

We tossed rocks at it, watching the flies buzz off it and then back on it. I noticed Tyler was putting all he had into his throws, like pitching a baseball as hard as he could, like he was really, really mad. I didn't say anything, figuring if he wanted to talk about it he would.

Our whole gang went back a couple days later, and the whole raccoon was now moving, writhing like it was alive. I grabbed a long stick and poked it hard from as far away as I could stand and still hold the stick. I poked a hole right through its fur and all of these nasty yellow maggots came flowing out of the hole. As they moved all over under its fur, they made it ripple. The stench, even worse now, filled the air again, and we took off running, laughing as hard as we could, though inside I felt bad for the poor raccoon.

Craig tripped and started to tumble down the hill. He kept sliding faster and faster, finally landing in the stream that flows under Tunnel Number One. All four of us looked at him, laughing and pointing. Then, one by one, we screamed "GERONIMO!" and hurled ourselves into the cool water below, trying to get the stink off of us.

CHAPTER NINETEEN

MEAN MRS. RICKLES

The water flowing in the ditch behind my house looked like a long spilt drink of chocolate milk splitting the neighborhood exactly in two and leading the "secret" way from our house on the hill down to Mean Mrs. Rickles, who tried her hardest to make everyone else's life miserable. The kids in the neighborhood had done some really mean things to her, but nothing had happened for awhile. Still, somehow I knew this wasn't over. This year Mean Mrs. Rickles would make us pay for the past, I just knew it.

For weeks, everyone in Skyview talked about her recent weird behavior and loud outbursts when kids would walk along the ditch behind her house and just how crazy Mean Mrs. Rickles was becoming. A storm was building.

There was a grassy oasis following the ditch line, and the houses were spread far apart with big green yards all backing up to the oasis. It was a great place to play and hang out. There were tunnels we crawled through full of crawdads, minnows, water skippers, frogs and a million small fish, but for some reason Mean Mrs. Rickles thought she owned it all.

Something about muddy water attracted us boys like honey does bees. Most of the folks along the ditch were quite friendly, and when they saw our band of boys coming their way they would nod, or ask about our parents, or share an apple or peach off one of their trees.

But there was one lady who was NEVER friendly: Mean Mrs. Rickles. She was about as unpleasant as a person gets. If she wasn't calling the sheriff about my dogs, she was calling my mom and dad about us trespassing on her land. No matter how many times my dad had told her that the wide strips of grass surrounding both sides of the ditch were community property, she still insisted we were trespassing.

She called my dad a lot; it was just too tempting to bother her. It was really fun to try to make the old crab mad. We would climb the cottonwood trees near her backyard, talking really loudly and spying on her as she huffily worked in her back garden, glancing our way every so often but unable to tell exactly where our voices were coming from because of the thick leaf cover. Tormenting Mean Mrs. Rickles was a favorite pastime of all of us kids.

One time Butch and I were on a super secret mission. We had to see what was going on in Mean Mrs. Rickles's backyard to plan our next prank, which I'll tell you about later.

We whispered all the way down the ditch from my house.

"Do you think there is anyway she could catch us?" Butch said, panting.

"Yeah, I do. That's why I think this is so stupid. She'll kill us if she catches us."

Just then, a fly flew up my nose. I put one thumb on the other nostril and did a farmer's blow to get rid of it.

"What the heck are you doing?"

"I got a fly up my nose."

Butch started laughing, "Peters, you're a mega-dork if there ever was one."

"Shut up."

"Make me!"

I made a loud farting noise. "Phhht, you're made, in the shade, like a glass of pee lemonade!"

Butch chuckled, "Back at you, you piece of pooh, stuck like mud in a jar of glue!"

"Same to you, you lame old dunce, if I told you twice, means I told you once," I retorted.

We could go on like this for days with all kinds of rhyming insults. It drove our big brothers absolutely crazy, which was our main point. Now we kept throwing insults back and forth all the way down the ditch. My back was getting sore from bending over so low to the ground, but I wanted to make sure Mean Mrs. Rickles didn't see us coming.

I snorted again. I could feel the fly moving toward my brain through my nose, and it was driving me crazy. Suddenly the thought that the very same fly might have been on the dead bloated raccoon or on a pile of dog poop somewhere and that it might lay maggots in my brain totally grossed me out. I started doing the farmer's blow so hard I almost blacked out.

"You are so weird! Hey, Peters, wanna spend the night tonight?"

"Hmmm, when we get back to my house, I'll go ask Mom if I can."
"You always say that," Butch groaned.
"Say what?"
"Chicken butt."
"Back at you with a load of chicken pooh!"
We finally got right behind Mean Mrs. Rickles's house.

"Shhh..." I put my fingers to my lips and motioned toward her backyard. She was standing in a tall grove of corn at the far reaches of her house. I felt a cold shiver go up my back. Just the sight of her scared me.

I knelt silently with Butch in the ditch behind her house looking through her chain link fence. She was talking with someone I figured was her husband, a man I had never really seen up close. We knew he lived there, but no one ever seemed to see him come or go much. It was weird; she was always around, and he was like a vapor or a shadow. I'd make myself scarce if she were my wife too; how embarrassing!

She was talking really loud, not knowing we were anywhere near. "The corn's ready. I'll pick it first thing tomorrow morning when the sun is rising to bring up the sugars. It'll be sweetest then, and this time those stupid kids aren't going to spoil it. I'm sleeping out on the screen porch tonight, and if I hear so much as a tiny noise, I'll break some heads!"

"Yes, dear," his meek male voice squeaked.

There's nothing like knowing the enemy's strategy. We were going to have to get some help if we were going to muck up her plans.

All of a sudden I went into a sneezing fit. The fly somehow had worked its way into the area between my eyes. I knew I was going to die right there from flymaggotbrainitis.

Butch held his hand over my mouth and nose. "Peters, knock it off, she's going to catch us!"

Just then, a huge sneeze escaped, drenching his hand. "GROSS!" Butch screamed.

I started laughing so hard I fell down in the ditch. But at least I had stopped sneezing. Somehow the last sneeze had sent the fly flying out of my nose.

There was an ongoing rite of passage in our neighborhood.

Every year a dare was thrown down at the streetlight, and someone had to prove their bravery by sneaking down the ditch and jumping into Mean Mrs. Rickles's backyard and stomping down her corn right before it was ready to harvest. It was mean, but she was meaner. There was only one year that that the plan didn't work and it had become a huge challenge to come up with a way to distract her. This year the dare had been thrown down to Butch and me by our older brothers, and everyone else thought it sounded like a good idea. Butch and I we were scared to death of Mean Mrs. Rickles, but we weren't about to admit that to anyone.

Last year, my brother and his friends had found out that Mean Mrs. Rickles and her husband were going to be gone for several days. How they found out they never told, but I knew they had been sneaking into her yard, stealing peaches off her trees, when they heard her planning.

Anyway, they waited a couple of days, making sure the coast was clear, before they turned on the water to both of her outside spigots that connected to her house and to the one out in her yard that pumped water from the ditch to irrigate her garden and yard. The water ran for several days on full blast before anyone noticed.

One of the neighbors must have eventually noticed, but it was too late: her whole back yard was flooded. Worse than that, I heard that her basement was flooded too. She was as mad as a hornet and made a big stink at the homeowners' board meeting in the fall about all of the juvenile delinquents in the neighborhood. She pointed a finger at my dad, and told him that she knew somehow that his sons were involved and she would get some evidence to prove it. I had nothing to do with it, and it made me mad when Dad sat Carl and me down to talk about it, as though we were both guilty. Well, it was payback time for her now.

Mean Mrs. Rickles had been growing a garden and trying to grow corn for as long as I could remember. Just about every year someone did something to ruin her corn crop. One year two of the older kids pulled up every single stalk right out of the ground and then floated them one by one down the ditch. Who knows where that corn ended up? Probably out in Kansas or somewhere like that. I always imagined that corn growing along the ditch for hundreds of miles feeding baby raccoons, skunks and other creatures. That made me happy, but not Mean Mrs. Rickles.

I watched Mean Mrs. Rickles's platinum-bottle blond-haired head bouncing toward the back screen leading into her house, and giggled nervously as I imagined the havoc we would cause that night. My stomach felt like it did when you fall a long way or go down the hill on a roller coaster. Mean Mrs. Rickles planned to sleep out on her screened porch to protect her precious corn, and that meant big danger for us. But I was so tired of being called "chicken" all the time that I was willing to take the risk, knowing that she might kill me. I couldn't back out.

Butch and I sneaked back up the ditch to plan our strategy under the tree where my tree house was. After we drew a map of our plan in the dirt ten times we climbed up into the tree house to plan the rest of our strategy.

I had a stash of huge jawbreakers in a paper bag that I had hidden under a branch at the edge of the tree house. Butch and I each sucked on one, comparing whose was getting smaller faster. They were too big to fit in our mouths, so we were both drooling all over our t-shirts. We got the brainy idea to hang our heads off one side of the tree house and have a contest to see who could make the biggest drool pool under the tree. After about fifteen minutes I was so dizzy from having my head upside down I declared Butch the winner, even though I thought my drool pool was bigger.

We planned to wait until hours after the streetlights flickered on, when the sun was long gone and it was pitch black out. No one would see us as we trampled down Mean Mrs. Rickles's corn.

At least, that is what we hoped. Our very lives depended on it.

Much later, it was just after midnight. All of us were supposed to be sleeping at each other's houses in our backyard tents, though Butch and I were the ones who had the job ahead of us. You see, we switched around from yard to yard in the summer so much, usually playing hide-and-seek or kick the can under the main streetlight until it was so late that our moms never really knew which tent we were going to sleep in. That was going to work out well for us on this particular night.

Butch and I sneaked out of my downstairs bathroom dressed in the darkest clothes we owned and with our faces blacked out with leftover Halloween face paint. We looked like soldiers in camouflage, and we were ready for our mission. Tonight we would prove to everyone that we had what it took.

"Butch, you scared?" I whispered.

"Nah. Who's scared of a mean old lady?" Butch said quickly, but I could hear fear in his voice.

"Yeah, me neither." I tried to sound convincing but butterflies were having a heyday in my stomach.

While Butch and I sneaked down the ditch to do the deed, Craig and Tyler were getting ready to blow off some M-80s and pop-bottle rockets in Mean Mrs. Rickles's front yard. Tyler said he was going to blow her mailbox up, but we were all pretty sure that was a big crime and that he could go to prison for doing that. He said he didn't care, that prison would be better than living in his house with his dad.

I really hoped he didn't blow up her mailbox. I didn't want him to go to prison.

The plan was that Carl and Kevin would stand at one end of Mars Boulevard, where Mean Mrs. Rickles lived, with a flashlight, while Tyler and Craig hid behind a car across the street from her house. At the other end of the street, which intersected with Mercury Avenue, were Greg and Kevin with another flashlight. If a car was coming they were to flash the flashlights three times in a row and everyone would go hide. To get things going, my brother was supposed to flash his flashlight once, Greg would return his flash once, then my brother would flash twice and when Greg flashed twice the fireworks would begin.

We were in position. I had a walkie-talkie, and my brother

had the other one. "Carl..." I whispered. No answer. "Carl..."
I whispered into the walkie-talkie again.

"GABE?"

I had forgotten to turn my volume down. His voice echoed
down the ditch.

Butch whispered loudly, "Peters, are you trying to do get us
killed?

I fumbled for the volume before my brother could say
anything and accidentally turned the squelch. A high-pitched
noise blasted out of the ditch.

"WHO'S THERE?" Mean Mrs. Rickles cried out from her back
screen porch.

Butch and I stood totally still. My heart was beating so
hard I was sure she could hear it.

"I SAID, WHO'S THERE?, I KNOW ITS YOU BOYS,
AND BELIEVE ME YOU ARE GOING TO BE SORRY IF YOU
TRESPASS ON MY YARD AGAIN! I'LL CALL THE SHERIFF
AND YOU'LL ALL END UP IN JUVENILE DETENTION!"

"NO!" my brother's voice echoed down the street. I could tell
he was trying to disguise his voice, making it a lot deeper than
it was, but he wasn't supposed to say anything; he was supposed
to do it all with the flashlight. He must have heard Mean Mrs.
Rickles screaming, and figured we were going to get caught
unless he created a diversion.

Butch grabbed my shoulder. I could feel his hand shaking.
"Man, we are so dead. Look!"

Mean Mrs. Rickles was coming across the backyard toward
us really fast. We started to climb out of the ditch to run as
fast as we could when suddenly an explosion of light and a huge
BOOOOM came from her front yard.

"WHAT THE..." Mean Mrs. Rickles turned. Her face lit up; she
was wearing curlers. "THOSE DOGGONE BRATS!" she started
hurtling toward the front yard.

"Oh my gosh, it worked!" Butch whispered. "Come on!" We
started a full-out run and then tried to jump the chain-link
fence at the back of her yard.

I fell over the fence trying to climb it too fast and landed on my face. "OW!"

"Get up, Peters! Hurry, before she comes back!"

Back porch lights all over the neighborhood were coming on like fireflies at dusk on a hot summer night. Houses started to light up inside, and it looked like a whole row of jack-o-lanterns coming alive. The firecrackers were waking up the entire neighborhood.

I panicked. If everyone was waking up, so would all of our parents, and they might come looking in the tents to make sure we were all home in our backyards.

We were in her corn in seconds, stomping and smashing and pulling and shredding and tearing. More explosions were lighting up the front yard. We could hear Mean Mrs. Rickles out there screaming into the dark, "YOU IDIOTS ARE IN BIG TROUBLE!" Butch and I were laughing and stomping so hard that we were totally out of breath.

I was totally terrified, but in the moment something took over me and made me a madman. We would be legends. We would be thought of as brave, like the older boys. Now no one could ever call me a chicken again. I stomped and pulled and laughed like I was going insane.

Butch grabbed two ears of corn, holding them up high in the air as he yelled, "LOOK, PETERS, SOUVENIRS! LETS GET OUT OF HERE!"

We ran to the fence and once again, I clumsily climbed over. This time my belt loop caught on one of the links and held me there. "Butch, HELP ME!"

"COME ON, PETERS!" Butch growled.

"STOP USING MY NAME!" I whispered a little too loudly.

"Sorry, Peters," Butch whispered back. "Come on!"

"I can't. My jeans are caught on the fence!" I whined.

"Just take them off!"

"No way man! I'm not leaving my pants here!"

"Come on! We're going to get caught!"

"Help me!"

Butch lunged at me and pulled my arms so hard I thought he was pulling my shoulders right out of the sockets.   A loud ripping sound filled the air and then I felt air on my butt. He had pulled me so hard that it had ripped off the belt loop and my back pocket and a big piece of my underwear, which were now hanging on the back of Mean Mrs. Rickles's fence.

We started running down the ditch line when I stopped hard. "Oh, my gosh Butch, if she finds my pocket she will know it's me!"

"HOW?"

"Think about it. She calls all of our moms and tells them about the pocket. My mom sees mine missing. I am dead!"

"Well, there's nothing we can do about it now!"

"I have to go back and get it!"

"Peters, no offense, but with your leg, you will never make it."

"I have to!" I insisted.

"Oh dangit, I'll go." Butch turned and ran as fast as he could back to the scene of the crime.

There hadn't been a firecracker blast for a few minutes.

Just as Butch started pulling on the pocket stuck on her fence, mean Mrs. Rickles came running into the backyard. She started screaming, "THOSE DARN BRATS! LOOK WHAT THEY DID TO MY CORN! THATS THE FINAL STRAW! I AM CALLING THE POLICE! EVERY LAST ONE OF YOU IS GOING TO JUVENILE! I KNOW WHO YOU ARE!" Her voice echoed through the entire neighborhood.

I stayed really low in the ditch, whispering to myself, "Butch, come on man, don't get caught, come on. I don't want to go to jail!" I started creeping low in the ditch trying to see what was going on.

Mean Mrs. Rickles was opening her gate; the squeaking noise filled the otherwise silent air.

"Come on Butch, where are you?" I couldn't see any sign of him, and just knew he was going to get caught.

All of a sudden, way down on the other end of the ditch and hidden by the huge trees from Mean Mrs. Rickles, I saw Butch running out onto the gravel road and disappearing.

Mean Mrs. Rickles didn't even see him, but now she was walking my way. My heart started beating really hard. The tunnel was just a few feet away but she was coming on fast. I got as low as I could in the ditch, which meant I was almost totally submerged in the water. The current pulled me right into the tunnel. I held on to the outside lip of the tube that went under the grass making the tunnel and steadied myself.

Now I was in the dark tunnel where she couldn't see me. I heard her stomping down the ditch looking for us and yelling at the top of her lungs. I stayed in the tunnel. She walked back down the ditch and stood right above me, probably looking up into the cottonwood trees. I could hear her breathing and saying unrepeatable things under her breath.

Finally she went back through her creaky gate and I could hear her inside her house yelling about calling the police. She was really steamed this time. She was probably most mad about us tricking her again more than anything, you had to be mad being outsmarted by a bunch of kids.

I sneaked down the ditch and got out in my backyard. Butch and the other guys were in our tent recalling every single moment of the night. They were all so glad and relieved to see me as I slid into the tent that they were slapping my back and giving me high fives. I had never felt like such a hero in all of my life. My brother even seemed proud of me. We howled with laughter until Mom came out and told us all to go to sleep.

The most amazing thing about the whole night was that even with all that noise, not one of our parents had come looking for us until my mom came out. I think they all liked the thought of Mean Mrs. Rickles getting back some of her own trouble.

Afterwards, my dad, as usual, being the great guy that he was, took Mean Mrs. Rickles a bag of corn and some other vegetables from our garden. He didn't want to ruffle her feathers so he left it on her porch. It made me feel both good and bad inside.

Somehow I think that I was one of the reasons he did it.

CHAPTER TWENTY

NOT MY BRIGHTEST IDEA

We were past the midpoint of summer and running out of new things to do. We fished most every day, and hung out up in the tree house. But we needed a change; we were getting bored.

Craig and I hung our feet in the ditch, floating milkweed pods and imagining them as boats in a race when I got an idea. The night before, we had flown our Cox airplanes under the streetlight, and I had gotten this crazy idea that we could tie grasshoppers into the small cockpits so we could have real live pilots.

"Hey Craig, you wanna help me catch some of those little green-and-red grasshoppers that hang out under the cottonwood tree near the ditch in my backyard?"

"Uh, yeah, I guess. How come?" he said, seemingly annoyed.

"I wanna see if we can tie them into the cockpit on my Cox airplane, and then fly it with them in it," I said excitedly, ignoring his attitude.

"What? Peters, you are so weird!"

"But it would be so cool to have a pilot!"

"Hmmm..."

I could tell Craig was getting interested.

"Well, we could try it. Wanna?"

"Sure. There's nothing better to do."

We walked around the house and caught four of the smaller-sized grasshoppers. We then took them into the garage, pulling the door down so no one could see us. I didn't know if my mom would think what we were doing was cruel and unusual punishment for a grasshopper, and I wasn't about to find out.

We were trying to figure out how to get them to stay in the small cockpit, but they just hopped out and disappeared under stuff in the garage.

Craig said, "Hey Peters, I know how we can get them to stay!"

"How?"

"Glue them in."

"Cool!"

We started looking around my dad's workbench and found some emblem glue that dad used to put the cool metal flames on my brother's go-cart.

"Try this!" I said.

Craig squirted a blob of it onto the little seat in my airplane and then pushed the grasshopper down on it, holding him for a while to make sure he stuck.

I grabbed this funny sprayer my dad has for bugs and weeds that you have to pump. It looks like a little machine gun, so I pointed it at Craig and pretended he was my prisoner. He wasn't too amused that I was goofing around while he was trying to make the grasshopper pilot thing work.

I pushed the sprayer up to Craig's face, screaming, "Chu must go wit me, you evil communist!" which was kind of funny, since I was the one using the Russian accent. Craig got storming mad when I accidentally shoved it too hard, hitting him in the nose and releasing some old bug spray. His nose began to gush blood and he started screaming that the toxic bug spray had lodged inside his nose and he couldn't shake it. He threw the garage door up and went screaming down my driveway toward home, spitting mad at me.

I muttered, "Well, at least you won't have any bugs in your nose."

As I turned around, Mom was standing there with her hands on her hips examining all of the mess Craig and I had made trying to work out the grasshopper pilot project. And for the rest of the day, I sat in that garage on Mom's orders cleaning out the garage and making sure everything looked better than when Craig and I had started. I was lucky she hadn't seen the grasshopper glued into the cockpit or I really would have gotten it.

I got kind of mad at Mom for wasting a perfectly good summer day, so I unplugged the freezer just to be ornery. I planned to plug it back in later on, but wanted to leave it unplugged just long enough for some of the ice to melt and maybe panic Mom. Dad always unplugged it when he defrosted it, so I figured it wouldn't really harm anything when water dripped out the bottom. It would be enough though to give Mom a scare when she went out there to get butter or something for dinner or Dad's favorite ice cream.

Dad came out after a while and told me I was done with my chore. The sun was setting by then, and I could hear my friends playing football down the way. Mom gave me the okay to go play with them, and I rushed down the street so fast I forgot all about the unplugged freezer.

That night Dad rewarded me for all of my hard work, and told me he wanted to talk to me about being mean to my best friend. He took me into town for a Dairy Queen cone, usually reserved for birthdays and other special occasions. So that night Mom didn't go to the freezer to get his favorite ice cream.

Nor did she go the next night, as we picnicked in the park at our annual neighborhood summer celebration.

As it turned out, no one had any reason to go into the freezer for several days.

But then my dad had to go to school to get ready for his fall classes. Early in the morning, as he was going to work, he slipped quietly into the garage as my brother and I slept in the rooms right above. He always tried to be quiet, but Mom called dad 'Thumbs,' because quiet wasn't what Dad did best. You see, Dad tripped on shadows and other things most of us step over. "The acorn doesn't fall far from the tree," he would say to me when I did something clumsy, which unfortunately was quite often.

That morning was no different. I could hear dad mumbling and fumbling around in the garage below. Suddenly he let out a loud, "PEEE-YOOOO! WHAT IS THAT SMELL?" A crashing sound came right through the floor, then "GABRIEL AND CARL PETERS, COME DOWN HERE!"

The meat in the freezer had begun to rot from being in a defrosted freezer for four days.

I bounded out of bed; my brother met me across the hall at his door. "Man, Dad sounds really steamed! What's wrong?"

I shrugged not yet knowing why dad was yelling and crept down the stairs. Carl was following close behind. By now Mom was up, and ahead of us.

When I stepped into the garage, the smell of the rotting meat, melted ice cream and other garage smells mixing became apparent. I knew at once that my little prank on Mom backfired.

Oh my gosh, I forgot to plug it back in, I shrieked inside my head. I was in for it — that I knew for sure.

On the ground, water, melted ice cream and popsicles and everything else that was liquid had seeped out of the freezer. Flies were buzzing over the mix, and there were a ton of them dancing and bumping themselves against the garage window. Dad was standing there holding the electric cord on the back of the freezer.

"Gabriel! Carl! Which one of you unplugged this?"

Carl said, "No way, Dad, I had nothing to do with it."

I just stood there speechless.

"Gabriel?"

"Uh, uh..."

"Gabriel Peters, what has gotten in to you lately? I got an earful from Mrs. Rickles about you boys. She is convinced you had something to do with her corn getting trampled, and now this?" Mom looked at me angrily.

"Uh, I uh..."

"Speak up, Gabriel, what happened?"

"Uh, uh..."

"STOP THAT!" Mom growled. "Tell us what happened."

"When you made me clean the garage, I got mad... as a joke I unplugged the freezer..."

"A joke? You think it is funny to waste all this food?"

"Uh, uh...no, I meant to plug it back in. I just wanted it to leak water, to scare you, and then you'd find out it was fine."

Mom shook her head and looked at Dad like he should do something.

"Gabe, you are a very lucky young man!" Dad declared.

"WHAT?" my brother and I said at the same time.

I am sure Carl was hoping I was going to get in really big trouble.

At Dad's comment, Mom was looking at him like he had lost his marbles.

"Well, I was planning on defrosting the freezer this week because we are getting our beef next week. We were down to a few packages of hamburger and some roasts, so there was hardly anything in there. If you had pulled a stunt like this with a freezer full, you would really be in big, big trouble."

"What? The Chicken-Squirt isn't going to get in trouble?" demanded Carl.

"I didn't say that, and Carl, this isn't your business. Go back upstairs," said Dad.

As Carl turned, and left, Dad instructed, "Gabe, I want this mess cleaned up. Throw everything in a plastic bag and seal it good, and then put it in the garbage can. Then scrub all that sticky popsicle mess out of the freezer and clean this floor up. When I get home I want this freezer and the floor to look shiny and new."

Mom was standing there, looked really disappointed in me, and that made me feel worse than anything. I didn't like it when she got mad at me, but her being disappointed in me was the worst feeling in the world.

"Also, young man," Dad added, "your allowance is going to pay for the food you spoiled. You better not try a prank like this again, do you understand me?"

"Yes Dad, I'm sorry..." My throat felt full and tears spilled out of my eyes. I felt so bad that Dad was angry with me.

I spent the whole day cleaning the mess I had made in the garage. It was the second wasted day cleaning the garage. I then did a thorough cleaning of my room. I pulled a ton of weeds in Dad's garden and picked vegetables. Then I helped Mom with a load of chores around the house trying to make it up to her. I was exhausted by the time Dad came home.

I was up in my room and could hear Mom and Dad talking in the kitchen. Dad came into my room and sat on the lower bunk. "Son, sometimes we do things we don't really mean to harm others, but they still do. Mom tells me that you worked really hard today, and what you did really looks great. It looks like with this week's allowance you will be all paid up."

Dad then gave me a big hug. I hugged him back and told him I would try to be better. Then I called Craig to see if we were still friends.

After Craig and I made up, I asked him if he wanted to come over. Mom and Dad had gone into town grocery shopping, and Mom had laid out some snacks for us on the kitchen counter. Craig and I sat watching Gilligan's Island on the TV and munching snacks.

I said, "What do you want to do?"

"I don't care. What do you want to do?"

After watching the rest of Gilligan and The Brady Bunch, we decided to taste a little of every single thing we found in our kitchens. We started in the refrigerator, which wasn't so bad, but when we hit the spice cabinet, we knew we were really in for some trouble.

Craig and I were always doing stuff like this. One time we ate so much rhubarb in the backyard that my tongue split open. He thought that was cool, and got mad that his didn't.

I could always depend on Craig to go along with my crazy ideas or to make up some of his own. That's what "almost" best friends do.

CHAPTER TWENTY ONE

TYLER AND KEVIN'S DAD

"YOU BROKE MY GLASSES, YOU JERK! YOU ARE GOING TO PAY FOR THOSE!"

My brother's friend Kevin had just thrown a ball as hard as he could at my face. It was weird; it didn't really hurt, but it sent my glasses spinning off onto the pavement, shattering one of the lenses and scratching the other one badly. It was a good thing that for once I had taken my mom's advice and worn my old pair to play.

"Pay for them yourself, you big baby!" he sneered. My friend Tyler was a pretty nice guy most of the time, except when his dad was being really mean, but his brother Kevin was always a jerk!

"Yeah, we'll see about that. I'll go ask my mom to call your mom and we'll see about that!" I started to storm off, but Kevin caught my arm and pinned it behind my back.

"You slipped and fell into the wall, Peters. You see, I had nothing to do with it. You got it?"

"What are you talking about? You know you did it."

Then I thought of the times both Kevin and Tyler had said that. They would show up with black eyes or a big bruise and when you asked them what happened, they would always say stuff like, "I tripped and fell."

"You rat me out and it will be the last thing you do." I could smell his breath on my face. It smelled like grilled cheese sandwiches, pickles and bacon, but not in a good, hungry-like way.

"WHATS THAT YOU SAID, KEVIN?" Carl's voice boomed. He had been behind Kevin's house, back at the ditch with a few buddies and was coming around the side of Kevin's house when he heard him threaten me. "I told you to lay off my brother. I'm sick of you picking on him." Carl shoved Kevin hard up against the basketball hoop, knocking him down.

"Get off it, Carl! You're always picking on him." Kevin got to his feet shakily.

"He's my brother, you idiot! I can pick on him, you can't!" Carl shoved him again, and this time added a hard punch on the shoulder.

Kevin came up with his fist clenched. "Peters, don't shove me, man. I swear I'll…"

It was weird. Tears filled Kevin's eyes when he was shouting at my brother.

"You swear what? Come on if you think you can take me," Carl growled.

Kevin was moving toward him when Carl dived on top of him and started punching him. Kevin started flailing his arms, trying to punch Carl and protect his face at the same time. They were rolling around the driveway when Kevin's dad came barreling to the front door. Seeing Kevin's dad made a cold feeling come over me, even though it was hot outside.

Standing in the doorway, his dad yelled, "KEVIN, WHATRE YOU DOING? PUNCH HIM BACK HARD, OR I'LL…" He was dressed in a pair of jeans, a dirty shirt and his big, fish-belly-white, hairy stomach hung over his belt. His hair looked like he had come out of a wind tunnel, and the look on his face was as angry as I had ever seen it.

Kevin and Carl were rolling around punching and jabbing at each other. Tyler peeked out the door under his dad's arm and started to laugh at the spectacle of our two older brothers fighting when his dad backhanded him hard.

"SHUT UP, YOU LITTLE IDIOT!"

Blood came spurting out of both of Tyler's nostrils. I wanted to turn and run, but was afraid that if I did his dad would come after me.

Tyler looked at his dad, cowering like a dog after he's been beaten once too many times. I felt so bad for him. He disappeared into the house. Pretty soon his mom came to the door and I could hear her yelling, "What did you do to Tyler?"

"NOTHING! JUST SHUT UP AND GO BACK INSIDE! YOU WANT ALL THE NEIGHBORS TO HEAR YOU?" he bellowed so loudly my brother and Kevin stopped fighting.

Kevin ran toward the front door. "Leave her alone!"

"Shut up! I didn't touch her! You get in this house right now! You let that Peters punk get the better of you, and I told you what happens when you don't win a fight!" His dad slapped Kevin hard on the back of the head.

"I HATE YOU!" Kevin screamed as his dad slammed the door shut.
Carl and I walked home in silence.

We could hear Kevin and Tyler screaming all the way down the block.

I didn't like Kevin much, but I couldn't remember ever feeling sorrier for someone than I did for him right then.

That night Tyler sneaked down to my backyard tent and crawled in next to me, his eyes full of tears and a blue bruise on his cheekbone. Carl and Kevin were down at the streetlight acting like nothing had happened, but I knew from that day on Kevin would never pick on me again.

Tyler was crying hard.

"What's wrong?"

He sniffled loudly, but wasn't able to talk yet. We sat there in the darkness for a long time. Finally he said, "My mom told me that we are leaving."

"What?"

"Mom's had it with Dad. She saw what he did to my face and said she can't take it anymore."

I turned on my flashlight and looked at Tyler's face. The whole side where his dad had hit him was puffy and blue and his eye was swollen shut. I felt sick to my stomach. "We are going to Iowa where my grandparents live. I may never come back. Mom said if we did, Dad would do something worse. My grandpa will protect us if Dad comes after us."

"When?" I felt sick.

"When Dad goes to work tomorrow we're all leaving."

"But..."

"It stinks, but we have no choice. Mom said Dad has been getting really angry so easy lately, and has been hitting her more and more. She's afraid soon he will do something much worse if she doesn't get us all out of here."

I wanted to cry. Tyler was one of the best friends I'd ever had. And I couldn't even understand how a dad could do that. My dad never, ever hit me, except for some spanks, but that was when I was really bad and I could always tell he hated even doing that.

"Gabe, I'm sorry about the way I've been acting...
I sometimes just feel so full of anger... Dad's been..."

"Come on, Tyler, don't worry about it. Man, I don't want
you to move at all."

"Me neither."

We sat there in the darkness for a long time. I felt really
bad for Tyler and his family. Now I had it even figured out
that that was why Kevin was such a jerk all the time. He was
tired of being picked on all the time and was taking it out on
the world. Why is the world so full of bullies?

When I woke up the next morning, I dug some worms and
went down to Tyler's backyard to his tent. We headed down to
Tunnel Number One with our fishing poles probably for the last
time ever. I never knew what it meant to be broken-hearted,
but something told me that the way I felt about losing one of
my best friends and how much I would worry about his dad
going after him was what it felt like.

I never told anyone about my broken glasses. I figured if
Kevin got in any trouble for that it would end up being a black
eye for him, so when Mom asked me some time later where they
were, I told her I had lost them fishing. Of course Mom made
me go to each of the tunnels to look for them, and then I got
a major lecture about how much stuff costs and I was lucky she
didn't make me buy a new pair. Even though Kevin was now
long gone, I still didn't want to tell.

Kevin and Tyler's house stood empty for a long time. I guess
when his dad figured out that his family was gone he just moved
on somewhere else. I was glad he was gone, but I really hoped he
hadn't gone to Iowa. Soon the bank put a sign in the yard and
a new family moved in. They had little kids who were too young to
play with us. They would never know that the initials carved in the
bark of the big cottonwood that hung over their backyard and the
ditch were the initials of the Secret Detective Brotherhood.

THE DAY THE CARNIVAL CAME TO TOWN

Every year, near the end of summer, the carnival came to town. It was always in this parking lot near the All Night Diner. My friends and I liked to sneak around near the trailers where the carnies live while they were on the road and dare each other to peek into the windows to see what they were doing.

Usually nothing was going on in them, but one time we saw The Fat Man eating a ton of hot dogs. He ate one right after another, totally raw, from the package, and he ate three packages while we were watching. That's like thirty hot dogs. Another time we saw the guy that runs the Tilt-A-Whirl kissing Jennie McNee.

Jennie was a high school girl with a bad reputation. I don't really know what that means, but it's what all the parents said when they talked about her.

We rode as many rides as we could afford and played the games, but when our money ran out we got as much entertainment watching the people who worked for the carnival.

Carnivals now always remind me of this weird guy who used to live in our downtown area until last summer. He was a guy who would keep popping up all over the place and sometimes I got the eerie feeling that he was following me. I even had a few nightmares for a while where he was chasing me around. Whenever we would go into town I would see him standing on the corner in front of the old post office with his bright, fiery-red long hair and really long mutton chop sideburns. He walked kind of like an orangutan, as though something was wrong with his legs. He was also only about four feet tall, a full-grown adult with a constant sneer on his face. I'd always cross the street to avoid his stare and had never heard a word come out of his mouth, but I would hear some grunts.

People who worked downtown passed him like they did the streetlights or the benches: not really seeming to give him much thought, as though they didn't even see him. I always wondered where he lived.

I stayed downtown really late one cold winter evening just before the holidays. The snowmen looked down from every street light and red and green plastic streamers hung from the wires with fake plastic wreaths over the two-way traffic. Everybody seemed a little happier because of the upcoming holidays. My mom would let me and Carl shop in the little stores all by ourselves so we could keep our Christmas presents a secret. Even though she told Carl to stay with me and keep an eye on me, he always took off and told me not to follow him.

Mom said she would be shopping at J C Penney and we would meet back in front of the post office in one hour. I was trying to buy something in a store for my dad. It came down to two things: some aftershave he liked, and a cool wooden backscratcher with a dragon carved on the handle. I didn't know which he would like more. I was thinking to myself, 'Maybe I should go ask Mom' when Carl grabbed the backscratcher out of my hand.

'Thanks Chicken-Little, that's just what I was looking for. Dad will just love it!' Carl sneered and went running off to the cash register. I guess that kind of made my decision easier.

I bought sweetly-scented candles for Mom, a bottle of Hai Karate aftershave and some razors for his straight edge for my dad.

But I wanted to buy my brother something he really wouldn't want. I needed to find the perfect dorky gift, and it takes a lot more thought to think of the perfect worst gift than it does to buy a nice one.

The weird little red-haired guy was on the corner as I left the candle store. The sky was getting pretty dark, and a cold breeze whipped down College Avenue, creating kind of a canyon that sucked the wind through real cold-like. I shivered and drew my coat closer to my chin. The red-haired guy sneered at me as I passed on the other side of the street and then he ducked in an alley behind an Italian restaurant. I watched him like the spies in my favorite movies, and wished my best bud Andy was there with me.

Just then he moved away from his spot. He started to walk

across the street toward me. I panicked, but if I ran he would see me. I held my body in tight to the brick doorway, which I had snuck into to spy on him.

He hobbled painfully past me and kept going. I decided to follow him, staying about a block behind him and trailing him dramatically, speaking into my wrist phone to the chief back at headquarters, just like Dick Tracy and other detectives, letting him know where the suspect was going next.

As he hobbled down block after block he came to the corner where St. Joseph Church is. He walked around the side that we school kids weren't allowed entry in, the same side the priests came and went from. He ducked into the door as I slinked quickly through the shadows to the door. I saw his wild red head retreat down the stairs into the basement where the potluck suppers and other meetings were held.

I crept down the stairs, trying to follow him. I could hear his shuffling footsteps retreating, and somehow he disappeared. I started to get scared thinking about being in that dark basement with him and rushed out, running down the street, back to College Avenue where Mom was already looking for me.

That year my buddies and I went to the carnival. We rode all of the rides and did some of the quarter toss games trying to win a big stuffed animal, and then headed toward the trailers where the carnies lived. Walking toward us, right down the middle aisle, was that same weird little red-haired guy. He was talking to another guy I saw around town.

"Yeah, I left with this carnival last year and this is the first time I've come back to town. I have seen the whole country. You ought to come with; it's really cool."

The other guy mumbled something, and then the red-haired guy pointed right at me and said loud enough for me to hear, "It's so strange. I see that weird-looking kid everywhere I go in this town. It's almost like he's following me."

I rushed out of there and ran as fast as I could down the sidewalk, with my friends following along as if I were playing some cool game that they wanted to be a part of.

CHAPTER TWENTY THREE
GADFLY PERONI

My friends and I had been trading comic books for a long time. My favorites were Batman, Superman, Spiderman and Archie. We sat up in the tree house and read the comics, imagining our superhuman strengths and how we would use them against our big brothers.

For Halloween last year, I got a really cool Superman costume with a plastic mask, but it didn't last too long with my constant tree climbing and running around the fields. I wish I had a real Superman outfit.

One kid that visited our neighborhood every year was named Gadfly Peroni. He had real superpowers. I swear Gadfly was his name; there's no making up a name like that, nor his powers.

One morning Gadfly called me into his backyard to show me his new Batman gloves. They had leather fringe and the famous symbol of the bat across the knuckles. Unless there's an occasion like a birthday, I wouldn't have gotten anything so cool from my parents, but this is Gadfly's grandmother's house, and when Gadfly came he got whatever he whined for.

When I first saw them, I thought about going into my house and acting like I had been crying. Then I could go ask Mom if there was any way I could have a pair of those cool gloves. But I was almost sure she would say no. Sometimes she said no, though, and then allowed it anyway. I guess she felt sorry for me, and that made me feel kind of bad, but not as bad as I felt not having those gloves.

I asked Gadfly if I could try them on. He coaxed me into the large grassy backyard and instead of letting me try on the gloves, he mentioned their ability to punch through bricks, then punched me so hard in the stomach I doubled up and fell on my back. I lay there writhing in pain, trying to pull air back into my lungs. He stood above me and laughed in the deep way a villain does.

The previous summer Gadfly, wearing the enviable Batman gloves, invited me to spend the night and go see a movie about Blackbeard's ghost with him and his grandma. We went to A & W and she got us each Mama burgers, onion rings and a huge frosty mug of their famous root beer. Gadfly coaxed me into the men's room and then proceeded to stuff the extra roll of toilet paper into the toilet. He held the flusher down until the whole bathroom was two inches deep in water.

We both walked out of there laughing at "our" little prank. A few moments later he was whispering in his grandmother's ear. She marched me to the manager where she explained that I had been the one to stuff the toilet paper into the toilet. I was speechless and ashamed, unable to speak to the towering man with the bald red face.

On the way home, I sat in the back seat quietly while Gadfly
sat in front with his grandmother slipping those Batman gloves
on and off his hands and glaring at me when his grandmother
wasn't looking, then smiling at her like he was all innocent.

When we got home Gadfly's grandmother pulled up to my
house and walked me up to the door. She explained to my
mother what had happened, and said I wasn't a good influence
on her grandson, so I wouldn't be spending that or any other
night at her house until I proved that I could be good. I was
really angry, but more relieved that I didn't have to hang around
with Gadfly all night. When we went into the house I told Mom
what really happened. She seemed to believe me.

Gadfly was going to leave in a week. I went down to his
grandmother's backyard and watched him from behind the tree
that hung out over the ditch. He was jumping on the trampoline
all alone, jabbing at the air with his Batman gloves. After a
little while he got bored with it and took the gloves off, tossing
them toward the fence that was just below where I was lying
against the branch so he couldn't see me. He went inside and
stayed in there, so I snuck down to leave.

I had been contemplating how best to get back at him for
tricking me at the A & W, and then I spied those gloves strewn
out across the grass. With the stealth of a spy in Russia, I
hopped over the fence hugging the trees and clutched the gloves
in my fingers. I slipped back into the recess of the yard and
as I neared the fence I heard, with great terror, Gadfly's
grandmother's voice. I froze for several minutes in place in
plain view, but somehow I was not seen; she was calling to
someone else in the house. I hastily jumped the fence and
ran all the way back home.

A little later, after I had felt the mock leather power as
I clenched and unclenched those gloves at the bathroom mirror,
I grew afraid of the punishment I might receive for stealing
them and tried to absolve myself by digging a hole to find
fishing worms. At the bottom of the hole I placed the
Batman gloves and covered them back up.

Within a few days Gadfly was threatening me with his brand-new pair of Batman gloves. I watched him coax my friend Craig into the yard and treated him to a breath-stopping stomach punching.

After he went back home from his grandmother's house, I thought of digging up the gloves and keeping them, but by then I really didn't want his gloves anyway. I knew if I ever got a cool pair of gloves like Gadfly's or any superpower's, I would use them on bad guys, not good guys like Craig. Bad guys like Gadfly.

CHAPTER TWENTY FOUR

DARE OFF

Andy finally came back home.

I had really missed my best friend a lot this whole summer. Usually he was only gone a month back east to see his grandparents, but this summer, for some reason, he was there almost the entire time with two of his brothers. There was something really wrong at home, but he didn't like to talk about it.

His grandparents lived in New York City and he always brought me something cool, like my Statue of Liberty piggy bank and the plastic placemat of the entire island of Manhattan. This time he brought me this cool pen with 'WALL STREET FORTUNES' written on it. It was see-through, and the insides were full of shredded hundred dollar bills. I guess the millionaires on Wall Street can afford to rip up their money and stuff it into pens.

Andy was the best friend a guy could ever have, and as soon as Andy was back, it was like he never left. We spent all day and night hanging out. We went from my tent to his, and during the day he and I fished and wandered through the old dumps and hung out in the tree house together talking about all the stuff we had been doing.

I thought I would never have another thing to do with Killer after my last run-in with him, but somehow I let myself get pulled into it (like so many other things) by my buddies. We were hanging around in the tree house talking about how much it stunk that Tyler was gone and trying to think of something to do when the idea of a dare-off came up. A dare-off is kind of like truth or dare, only with no truths. It is all about daring each other to do insane things.

From the tree house we could see Killer lying in a sliver of shade at the end of his long gravel driveway, as he did every day, waiting to devour a kid who might not realize that he still had another two feet of chain he could use to lunge at him.

It started with a simple dare: to run within an inch of where we thought Killer's chain ended and make a huge screaming noise at him to wake him up. Andy did that, and scared himself so badly when Killer came lunging about an inch closer than he had expected.

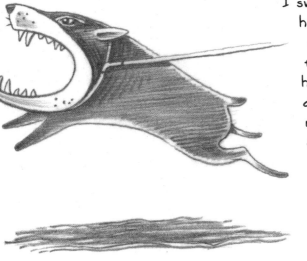

"You you c-c-could smell the b-b-blood on his breath! I swear h-h-he must have j-j-just eaten a k-k-kid, 'cause that's w-w-what he smells like." Andy always stuttered more when he was excited or scared.

"How do you know what kid blood smells like?" we all asked.

Andy just sputtered, sweat was pouring down his face on account of being so nervous. Next Andy got to dare someone. He dared Craig to jump the fence on the side of Killer's yard, creep across until he was up by the house and then scream for Killer, who would for sure run at him. He had to make it all the way to the other side of the yard before Killer could eat him alive. Craig crept in there and did it somehow. We all were terrified we would never see him again.

It was Andy's idea to hide in the ditch across the street from Killer's house to get a better view of the dares. Killer was so mad, he snarled and slobbered, lunging the whole time, trying to get at us. He glared at us all with blood-red eyes as we lay on our stomachs across the road in the ditch.

I was afraid that the dares were going to escalate to the point that I would have to go up to Killer's owner's front door, and there was just about anything I would do before that. Sure enough, the dares kept getting scarier and scarier until the worst dare of all came.

It was my turn, but then Andy said, "G-G-G-Gabe shouldn't d-d-do this one. His leg c-c-could cause some p-problems, s-so let's l-l-let him out of this one."

"No, I'm okay!" I said, like I was mad that they weren't going to dare me to do it too. But inside I was so relieved, I winked at Andy. He winked back at me. What a great guy! He always was watching out for me.

So the dares had come back around to Craig. He had to run across the road and sing "Happy Birthday to Killer" in an opera voice at the top of his lungs. But Killer just glared at him; he didn't even lunge once at him.

Craig then came across the road and pointed at Eddie, who he was mad at for calling him names. Craig dared Eddie to paint Killer's butt with hot sauce.

Eddie's lip started trembling, his hands shaking. "I QUIT!"

Eddie had given up. I had never seen him do that before. We all got a great laugh out of the dare, though, imagining someone being so stupid to try that one on Killer. Eddie swore he was going to do it someday.

Now, when someone quits on a dare-off, they have to do three other things someone tells them to on another dare. Those things were usually worse, and the rules and location were changed for the next dare-off. As we were trying to think of the next dares, my dumb brother and his friends came up to us.

"What are you sissy boys doing?" Carl asked.

"Dare Off, and Eddie just quit," I said.

"Oh man, let's think of three really good ones this time," Eddie's big brother snarled to our older brothers. They followed us around and decided they were going to play too. There wasn't anything we could do to stop them.

Eddie's brother had made my brother do an ultra-dare once (meaning involving an adult, which almost always backfired and got you grounded.) Carl had to run down the ditch behind our houses right when the sun was going down almost naked. It was so dumb. The older boys called it "streaking", which is the same thing as just running around naked. You can get in a lot of trouble for running around naked.

Mean Mrs. Rickles is always in her garden at that time of night, and the dare required him to scream extra loud when he passed behind her house. The idea was that he was going to wrap his t-shirt around his head so she wouldn't know who he was, and then scream at the top of his lungs at her.

My brother never turned a dare down, and the prize if he did it was that we all would buy him a candy bar up at the bait shop. Yet my brother spent his whole life grounded for doing stupid stuff, and there was nothing stupider than messing around with Mean Mrs. Rickles.

As soon as it started to get dark, he climbed up into the tree house and took his clothes off. He climbed back down in his tighty-whities as all of the boys started to chant, "TAKE THEM OFF!" "T-T-TAKE THEM OFF!" "TAKE THEM OFF!"

"THIS IS GOING TO BACKFIRE BIG. I JUST KNOW IT!" I yelled.

My brother called me a chicken-worrywart and stripped off down to his underwear. He pulled an extra pair of tighty whities out of his jeans pocket and wrapped them around his face like a mask, looking out the front pee-hole as he started screaming and running. He ran down the ditch line with all of us following behind him, laughing so hard we could hardly stand up.

He stopped screaming and snuck up right behind Mean Mrs. Rickles's house, ducking into the tunnel and spying on Mean Mrs. Rickles hoeing in her garden. The rest of us were hiding behind the cottonwood trees, whispering and laughing our heads off and wondering what my brother was up to. Somehow I knew he was going to do something really stupid, just to get a bigger reaction since he had an audience.

As we waited to see what Carl was going to do, I started thinking about the time last summer when Mean Mrs. Rickles was in her front yard and a bunch of us guys were riding wheelies on our stingrays. Craig pulled up on his handlebars right in front of Mean Mrs. Rickles's, all show-offy like he was going to ride a wheelie for a block when he crashed right into her car IN HER DRIVEWAY! Mean Mrs. Rickles bolted out of her yard, screaming and yelling at all of us. Craig was bleeding, and she ran right past him like it didn't matter. Instead of helping him even a little bit, she just yelled at him and then called his mother. Craig's mom wasn't the nicest lady anyhow, but having Mean Mrs. Rickles call screaming about what a total idiot he was didn't help.

My brother suddenly started screaming at the top of his lungs,

popping out of the ditch wet, muddy and looking naked with his
underwear over his head. Mean Mrs. Rickles turned around just
in time to see him flying over her fence. It startled her so badly
that she started running toward her house as my brother trampled
all over her garden, screaming like a madman.

All the guys were rolling around on the ground laughing as hard
as they could. Kevin said Mean Mrs. Rickles was so scared and
startled she had fainted, but no one really believed him.

My brother was running in circles using his tighty-whities now
as a lasso over his head. The porch light came on, and Mr. Rickles
started yelling at the top of his lungs. He came lunging out of the
house, and it caught everyone off guard.

My brother pitched his extra underwear toward the house,
screaming like a wild Indian, and ran back out of the yard,
bounding over the fence, and running all the way back to the
tree house. By the time we caught up with him, we were totally
out of breath, almost unable to breathe from laughing so hard.

We rolled around laughing all night long, remembering and
bringing up points over and over about how funny it was. You
could hear the phone ring in my house across the street when you
were in the tree house, and we all waited for Mean Mrs. Rickles
to call my mom. She didn't.

My brother somehow had gotten away with it. We all owed him
a candy bar, which meant the next day he would have eight candy
bars. He was lucky, lucky, lucky.

The next morning the doorbell rang. I looked out my bedroom
window at Mean Mrs. Rickles standing on our porch. She looked
totally angry. My mom went to the door and Mean Mrs. Rickles
handed my mom my brother's tighty-whities with his name written
in permanent ink on the waistband.

Carl got grounded for two weeks, and he had to spend an hour
every day helping Mean Mrs. Rickles fix her garden back up. But
he did get all of those candy bars, so I didn't feel too bad for him.

I told him, "I'm going to go ask Mom if I can have those candy
bars since you are in trouble."

Carl punched me, so I didn't.

Back to the ultra-dare for Eddie. He ended up having to call Mean Mrs. Rickles while we all listened in on Eddie's dad's speakerphone. He read from a script we had written out for him.

Her mean, acidic voice came on after three rings, "HELLO?"

"Hello, this is Stanley Snerts with Sears..."

"YES?"

"Just a few questions, ma'am..."

"I don't have time to answer your questions..."

"Is your refrigerator running?"

"Of course it is..." her voice sounded suspicious and as usual, angry.

"Well, you better run after it, because it just ran by my house! Ha, ha, in your face! I GOT YOU, MEAN MRS. RICKLES! TAKE THAT, YOU OLD WITCH!" He slammed down the phone, and we all busted a gut laughing so hard.

Within seconds the phone was ringing. Mean Mrs. Rickles was going down the list of "evil boys" in the neighborhood trying to catch us. We all high-tailed it out Eddie's backdoor, leaving him holding the bag when his mother started asking questions.

The second dare was to ring-and-run or doorbell ditch or porch player, which boils down to going onto someone's private property and knocking on the door or ringing the doorbell and then running as fast as you can and hiding. Usually several rounds a night are played on the same house, which gets really daring when you can see people peeking out of their windows from behind their curtains, thinking you can't see them.

The dare was to ring-and-run Mr. Reentz, a fifth grade teacher at Eddie's school. Not once but ten ring-and-runs in a row without getting caught. If you got caught, you had to ring-and-run another person ten times without getting caught.

Mr. Reentz was a nice guy, but no one was nice after being ring-and-rung ten times. On ring number five we could see Mrs. Reentz peeking out the upstairs window as Mr. Reentz hid on the side of the house, waiting. Right as Eddie was hitting the porch, Mr. Reentz came running out and chased Eddie down the street. I wouldn't want to be in that parent teacher conference come fall.

But Eddie still had to ring-and-run someone ten times without getting caught. We thought about Mean Mrs. Rickles, but then Andy suggested the crazy old lady who lives up on the hill in the haunted house. That would have to wait, though, for more reasons than I can go into right now.

The last dare Eddie had to complete was the one that horrified him more than anything. He had to knock on Lauren Warner's door and, when she came to the door, sing love songs to her. Lauren was like the cutest girl ever, and we were all really afraid to talk to her.

We were all across the street watching Eddie singing, "My eyes adored you... When I first laid eyes on you I knew... You light up my life... I have loved you since..."

The weird thing is that she just stood there smiling the whole time. When he was done she pulled him inside and shut the door.

What really stunk was that she was so impressed with Eddie's bravery that she became his girlfriend. Who would have ever seen that one coming? Eddie and Lauren??

CHAPTER TWENTY FIVE

TIMES, THEY ARE A-CHANGING

The summer was going by pretty fast, and I had a feeling things were going to be different for me at school next year. For one thing, my personal bully/bodyguard, Ronnie, wasn't going to be picking on me. His friends had moved on too, so I actually was not afraid to go back to school for the first time in my life.

The whole gang of kids from the neighborhood were playing hide-and-seek, and I was going to hide in my favorite spot surrounded by the three apple trees across the ditch from Mean Mrs. Rickles' house. I had never been caught there.

I usually snuck out to run to home base, or when someone fast was up, I'd just sit there until they yelled "Ollie-Ollie-in-come-free" - on account of my leg and not being able to run that fast. Then I'd jump Craig's fence and come out through his front gate. No one ever figured my hiding place out, and when they tried to follow me, I'd just find a different place instead so they would never know about the best place to hide of all.

I was running along in Craig's backyard, and there was a place where you had to jump over the four stacked railroad ties that made up a wall to miss Craig's mom's garden. I usually had to stop and pull myself up, because I couldn't jump the whole thing on account of my leg.

But this particular night, when I was getting ready to pull myself up, I was able to just hop up on top of it. I also had a better run going into it, too. I often couldn't get enough of a run too because I hobbled so much, but I was running better than I ever had before without my built-up shoe on.

The next time it was time to hide I tried it again, and found I could jump it again. It surprised me, because I had my PF Flyers on instead of my built-up shoe which I always wore when I was playing. So I asked Craig to run behind me to tell me if I was running better than usual to him, too.

'CHECK IT OUT, GABE! MAN, YOU'RE A SPEED DEMON! YOU AREN'T HOBBLING AS MUCH!' Craig started whooping and yelling at the top of his lungs, and on account of all the

noise he was making Butch caught us and we had to do rock, papers, scissors to decide which of us had to seek next. But Craig was excited because he said he had never seen me run so well. All the other kids gathered around and asked me to run so they could watch, too. Some said they saw nothing different, but most of them thought there was something. I could tell something was very different.

When I got home I took out mom's sewing basket. "I have to go ask Mom..." I said to myself. I then asked her to measure my legs with her tape measure.

I had done this a million times since Dr. Rumley told me my legs would most likely be the same length at some point since the bone that was so curved was slowly straightening out. But Mom always tried to get out of measuring my leg; I think it was hard for her to see how sad I got when there was no change. This night, though, when she was measuring she started sniffling.

"Mom, what's wrong?"

Mom looked up at me. A tear was moving down her cheek and that made me feel kind of sad. "Gabey, your leg has grown out a quarter inch. That's the closest they've ever been."

I hugged Mom and started crying too. She held me in her lap for a while, and then I whispered, "Mom, I'm sorry I'm not as good as your own son might have been. Do you ever want to take me back?"

Mom looked at me and started crying harder. She took my shoulders in her hands and squeezed firm. "Gabriel Peters, what on earth are you talking about? You are my own son. You are the best son any mom could ask for. Why would you say such a thing?"

"I'm sorry, Mom, I didn't mean anything bad. I just feel bad that you got stuck with a kid with a short leg and bad eyes. I'm such a worthless geek. You and Dad would have made a better kid." I tried to smile.

"Who filled your head with that nonsense? You are a smart, handsome, wonderful boy. You show me one person who doesn't have something different about them. Look at the way my front teeth are split." Mom's voice sounded mad, but I could tell by the tone that it wasn't me she was mad at.

"I just meant..."

Mom was stroking my hair and I crawled up into her lap.

"Gabe, you are the boy I hoped and prayed for. You are exactly what I wanted. I wouldn't want you to be any different than you are."

"Will you still like me as much when my leg grows out and I'm more normal?"

"Gabey baby, you will never be normal," Carl sneered sarcastically. He'd been watching us and not understanding what was going on.

"Carl, go brush your teeth and get to bed. I am talking to Gabe right now." Mom sounded angry.

Carl muttered something under his breath and shuffled down the hall.

"Gabe, I want more than anything in the world for your leg to grow and for you to run like all the other children on the playground, but I want that for you, not for me. I don't mind your wobble. I like the way you walk. I like to watch you when you are out in the fields. The fact that your leg is shorter doesn't change how I or your father feel about you at all."

"I know you love me, but I am such a geek, really, Mom. Look at me. I look like I have a ferret stapled to my head instead of hair, and I wear Coke bottle bottoms instead of glasses, and I limp. I hate the way I look. Everyone makes fun of me all the time. I hate it!"

"Gabey, someone else has filled your head with garbage, and that makes me mad." Mom's eyes were wet, and I kind of felt bad for making her feel sad again.

"Mom, look at me! I am a four-eyed geekaziod!"

"You are NOT a geek! I'll tell you what... If you can take care of your glasses for three months straight... I mean no broken frames, no scratched-up lenses, no problems at all, I will take you to the Optometrist and get you some of those cool wire-framed aviator glasses you like so much. And by then, who knows what your leg might do? And as for that hair, I think it is time your father stops cutting it and we take you to a real barber. How's that sound?"

"Are you serious? I can get the aviator wire-frames, for real? But I thought they're too expensive, Mom?"

"Gabey, some things are worth it, and you are worth every penny. We may not eat for three months, but you'll get those glasses if you take care of these you have on here."

"No, Mom, that's okay," I responded, startled. I didn't want my family to starve! "I don't want that..."

"I'm kidding you. We can afford to get you those glasses. But you have to take good care of these, I mean it."

"I know, Mom, I will." I hugged Mom tighter than I ever had. I couldn't believe it. Maybe things were really going to get better for me soon. Next year, if my leg kept stretching, I would win ALL of the Field Day events! (If only...)

My right leg had been one and three quarter inches longer than my left leg, or it had been that way for the previous two years anyway. Now Mom says it is only one and a half inches longer now. Soon they would be the same length like everyone else's.

CHAPTER TWENTY SIX
ANDY'S DAD

Carl and his dumb friends collected baseball cards and spent hours on boring hours trading them and talking about statistics and all this stuff that would put a normal person to sleep. I'm with Mom; she says, "Baseball is boring enough; why on earth would anyone want to know so much about all that technical stuff?" I mean, Carl kept his cards in order, by team and by position, and then alphabetically! He actually made cards to keep his cards in order.

Sometimes when Carl made me super-mad I shuffled his cards all out of order. I knew he would pummel me once I did it, but it is so funny watching him frantically working to get them back in order. He was totally obsessed.

Once Carl thought he could outsmart me by hiding them in his closet under a ton of dirty clothes, but I found them. Then he hid them in the crawlspace in a box labeled "dishes", but I found them. He even put a padlock on an old chest out in the garage and hid the key above the door going into the house, but I found it. He wouldn't tell on me, because that would be admitting that he couldn't handle his little brother, so I was able to keep doing stuff to them. I always wondered why it didn't occur to him that I would stop if he did something to my hot rod cards.

My buddies and I collected hot rod trading cards, the kind with some ridiculous souped-up hot rod and a drooling humanoid monster busting out of the top of the car. The smell of the pink bubblegum with its powdery bitterness coming off the card reminded me of the way the Russian Olive trees my mom had planted in our back garden smelled when they were blooming.

I had a huge collection of cards, and only traded when I had doubles. I had given Andy a few cards that he really, really wanted that I didn't have doubles of on account of, he was a Ford guy and I as a Chevy guy, and he was my best friend after all.

Andy and I sat in the garage spreading the cards out, imagining ourselves building a real hot rod someday. In Cub Scouts we had a derby race. We got a block of wood and model paint. Most of the cars kids raced looked like blocks that had been painted, but I always tried to make mine look like my hot rod car stickers.

I didn't have any great carving talent, but my cars always looked like the thing I was trying to replicate, at least to me.

Andy's cars were always the coolest though. He could draw really well, and drew the monster guys on his cars.

We also collected cool hot rod stickers that covered our school notebooks.

Andy's whole name is Andrew Isaac Epstein. His nickname used to be 'vowel' on account of his initials, but he asked us to stop calling him that. His mom is the only one who calls him Andrew; everyone else just calls him Andy.

Andy was the youngest boy of five brothers, and got picked on a lot. Andy has bright, I mean electric bright, red hair, and is tall for his age and really, really skinny. So we looked funny when we walked together. I mean, here would come a kid who was really small for his age, had a limp and was made fun of by anyone he passed walking along with a carrot top an entire head taller with the palest skin you'd ever see, and who stuttered when he talked to people who made him nervous — which was everyone but me and some of the members of his huge family.

My best friend Andy was from the only Jewish family in our neighborhood. His father was a barber and raised Afghan hounds and was usually pretty mean. He drank too much, according to my mom, and that made him nasty.

Sometimes there was what seemed like a hundred of those big, hairy dogs at any time in their backyard, which was surrounded by the tallest fence I had ever seen, to keep the dogs from jumping out. Andy's clothes were always covered with long, multi-colored hair, and he smelled like dog chow and dog poop on account of the fact that his dad made him and his brothers scoop the stuff up all the time. Of course everyone made fun of Andy because of that.

I get so mad when people made fun of people for things they can't change.

Andy was really mad at his dad and told me he was going to stick a bunch of hot rod stickers all over the side of his dad's car. His dad's pride and joy was a long, silver Cadillac.

Andy was using only the hot rod stickers that he had duplicates of. We were in his garage, and I tried to talk Andy out of it. I don't remember exactly how his dad came to find us in the middle of doing it because everything was in slow motion, but he had come out to the garage to get something, I suppose, and found Andy adhering sticker number 75 to the side of the 'Silver Star... I couldn't believe how many stickers Andy was wasting, but he was really, really mad about something he wouldn't talk about.

Suddenly, Andy's dad grabbed him really hard and threw him against the wall. Andy's nose started to bleed and I got super-scared that his dad was going to come for me next. But I was paralyzed. In my mind I wanted to get up and throw Andy's dad across the garage, but nothing on my body worked.

Andy was so mad and startled that he didn't even cry. He just looked at his dad with this really weird expression on his face. I'm not sure what hate looks like, but I think that is what I saw on Andy's face. That scared me more than anything. It made me think about Tyler and Kevin and their awful dad and that scared me even more. I didn't know what I would do if Andy moved away.

Andy's dad turned and growled at me. "Get out of here, Peters!"

I started for the door, but tripped.

"Oh, you poor little gimp! Why don't you learn how to walk like a normal kid?" Andy's dad sneered.

I thought to myself, "I need to go ask Mom what a gimp really is." So many people say that word to me, and all I know is it isn't meant to be nice.

"YOU'RE AN ID-DIOT!" Andy yelled, "D-d-don't talk to him l-l-like t-t-that! C-c-come on, G-Gabe, l-l-let's get out of h-h-here!" Andy helped me up, his nose still streaming blood. "I HATE Y-Y-YOU!" he screamed at his dad.

"YOU GET BACK HERE AND TAKE THESE STICKERS OFF MY CAR, YOU STUPID KIDS!" his dad yelled as we ran up the road toward my house.

"G-G-GO TO H-H!"

I clapped my hand over Andy's mouth before he got killed. I couldn't believe how he had just talked to his dad.

"I h-h-hate him w-when he d-d-drinks," Andy sniffled. "What really m-m-makes me m-m-mad is h-h-he w-won't even r-r-remember this t-tomorrow b-but I s-sure will!"

We climbed up into the tree house. Andy was crying hard and wiping the blood and tears off of his face with his sleeve. "I d-d-don't ever w-want to g-go back there again!"

"Come on Andy, stop talking like that. It will be okay." I was so afraid that the same thing would happen to Andy that had happened to Tyler. I knew it was selfish, but I was worried about losing both of the very best friends I ever had.

We were up in the tree house for a long time when Andy's big brother peeked up into the entrance. "Man, you are in so much trouble. Dad is really steaming!"

"I d-don't care! Just get out of here, c-creep."

I found out later that Andy's brothers had gone out into the garage and removed each sticker from his dad's car to keep him from getting into too much trouble. They were usually mean to Andy, but they must have known something really terrible would have happened to him if they didn't help him.

Older brothers can be so confusing. Just when you think you can't stand them and never want them around, they go and do something like that to protect you or to make sure other bullies don't pick on you. Carl is always doing stuff like that. It's confusing.

CHAPTER TWENTY SEVEN
MY BIRTHDAY

Since it comes in August, my birthday party was always the last party of the summer in our neighborhood. My mom usually baked my favorite German Chocolate cake and got tons of ice cream. Every kid in the neighborhood was invited to come.

My aunt Mary always sent me a drawing kit for my birthday. Every year since I can remember I got this same drawing kit. I mean, it's like she bought out a store or something and keeps them in her closet to send to her nephews every birthday and every Christmas. I swear, I would get two identical gifts from her every single year. I had about ten hundred of them in my closet up on the shelf!

The kit had this picture of a kitten on the metal box playing with a ball of yarn. I mean that was okay when I was a little kid, but it was pretty silly now. The sad thing about it was that it wasn't really a very good drawing kit. There were some silly pictures you were supposed to copy to learn to draw, and there were three kinds of pencils in them with lead that broke every time you pressed hard to make shadows on monsters or whatever. But it was better than what my friend Butch got from his grandma every Christmas. She sent him funny pajamas that she made out of burlap sacks and dryer lint that she glued on them. Last year he got one that was yellow, like Big Bird, and had chicken-looking feet in them. It was hilarious. The year before he got a blue animal that no one could identify. It looked like a cross between a pig and a cow. Butch wore it for Halloween, and we all got a good laugh out of it.

When he got the present, Butch's mom always marched him and his two brothers out into their backyard to take pictures in their Big Bird or cow-pig pajamas. So a drawing kit was okay, I guess.

Anyway, on my birthday this year I got a cool camera and tons of film from Mom and Dad. I told Dad that I wanted

to be a wildlife photographer when I grew up, like the ones in
National Geographic, where the photographer travels all over the
world. So this was my start. Little did I know that some of
the best pictures that camera would ever take would be at my
own birthday party.

About half an hour after the party started the doorbell rang,
three times in a row real quick and then another three times,
like the person on the other side of the door was
super-impatient or something. Mom told me to answer it,
thinking maybe a birthday package was arriving for me. I
bolted for the door. As I swung it open, my mouth dropped open.
I couldn't believe my eyes. Standing on my front porch in a
goofy blue short suit with a tie and shiny black shoes, holding
an unwrapped book I could only assume was a birthday gift,
was Ryan Rickles and his mother, Mean Mrs. Rickles.

"What are you doing here?" I sneered, I didn't really know
Ryan Rickles, but anyone related to Mean Mrs. Rickles had to
be a complete loser.

"Gabriel, don't be rude." My mom pushed past me, holding
her hand out to Ryan. "Would you like to come in?" she said
to Mean Mrs. Rickles.

Mean Mrs. Rickles just sniffed angrily at my mom, turned
and started to walk down the front sidewalk. She spun around
and glared at me, "I will be back in two hours to pick up Ryan,"
she growled.

Mom held the door open as Ryan pushed past me and went
to the corner of the living room, crouching low behind the couch
like a scared rabbit. I just shrugged and went to the backyard
where my real friends were gathered, leaving him there. Ryan
stayed there while we played games in the backyard, and no
matter how many times my mom asked him to come out back
he refused. I had no idea why Mom had invited him to my
party. None of the other kids even really knew anything about
him and his mother was our sworn arch-enemy. He almost
never left his yard and stood alone at the bus stop all the time,

I mean I couldn't remember if I had ever even heard him speak. Mom made me go in and ask him to come join us in a game of Lawn Darts, but he just stood there staring blankly into the wall, like my house was the last place on earth he would ever want to be.

Finally, when we were sitting down to have birthday cake, Ryan came out in the backyard. Everyone just stared at him as mutters filled the yard... "What's he doing here?"... "Who invited the weirdo?"... "Oh, brother, it's nose picker Rickles!"...

Jimmy, Butch's older brother, and Carl's buddy, pointed a lawn dart at him menacingly and pretended to hurl it at his forehead. Against my objections, Mom had invited Jimmy so my brother would have someone to hang out with at my party. Jimmy's voice boomed over all the others as he called out, "Hey Rickles, how come your mom is such a psycho nutcase?"

"JIMMY! THAT'S NOT NICE!" Mom snapped.

"Well, she is, jeez! Shut up, Mrs. Peters..." Jimmy growled. He said it under his breath, but it was a little too loud anyway.

Butch and Tony looked at each other in shock. Craig pushed his way forward to see the action going on, and Butch climbed up into the crotch of the cottonwood tree, somehow knowing fireworks were about to begin.

"What did you just say, Jimmy?" Mom asked, starting toward him.

Just then Ryan stood up and cut my mom off. He stood a full foot shorter than Jimmy. "What did you say about my mom?" Everyone looked stunned. The kid never talked and now when he spoke up it was to one of the biggest bullies in the neighborhood.

"I SAID SHE WAS A PSYCHO, YOU NOSE PICKIN WEIRDO!" As Jimmy looked around at everyone, laughing like he had just said the funniest thing ever, Ryan ran with all his strength right into Jimmy's stomach, sending him reeling backwards and down into the muddy ditch water.

Jimmy tripped and fell backwards, coming up screaming, "Rickles, you are SO dead!", but Ryan took a flying dive into the ditch and was on top of him like a wild dog, flailing his arms, screaming and slobbering all over him. They rolled around until both of them were soaked from the muddy water. Everyone was chanting, "NOSE PICKER!, NOSE PICKER!" Mom was screaming for them to stop, but Ryan had a firm grip on Jimmy's hair, and was trying to pull his head underwater. He was going nuts.

All my friends were howling and taunting Jimmy, who at one time or another had picked on them. We all enjoyed seeing Jimmy getting some of his own medicine from the most unlikely person in our neighborhood.

Meanwhile, Butch was yelling at his brother Jimmy to leave Ryan alone, but little nosepicking Ryan Rickles seemed to be getting the best of Jimmy as their fight grew. As a matter of fact, Jimmy was the one with a bloody nose now, not Ryan.

I ran to the kitchen table and got my new camera, and sprinted back to the ditch. I started taking pictures. My mom was still yelling at Jimmy and Ryan, but they totally ignored her and she wasn't about to get in the middle of it with them down in the ditch.

Except for Carl and my mom, we were all now chanting, "RYAN RICKLES!, RYAN RICKLES!", when suddenly from the corner of my eye I saw Mean Mrs. Rickles flying up the ditch that led between our houses.

Butterflies filled my stomach and I hid behind the huge cottonwood tree as Mrs. Rickles came storming into our yard. Her nostrils were flaring and she was spitting as she screamed, "WHAT IN GOD'S NAME ARE YOU DOING TO MY SON?"

Everyone stood there totally stunned at what was taking place. My mom looked helpless.

I snapped a few pictures of Mean Mrs. Rickles' snarling face as she stormed into my backyard and threw herself down into the ditch with Ryan and Jimmy, tossing Jimmy aside like a rag doll, she then slapped him hard across the face, screaming

"YOU LITTLE BEAST! KEEP YOUR HANDS OFF OF MY SON!"
Jimmy looked shocked, but kept flailing his arms at Ryan who
was now trying to scramble up the other side of the ditch.

My mom was waving her arm at me wildly, signaling for me
to stop taking pictures.

"Eunice, what are you doing? You can't treat a child that way!"
Mom barked.

Mean Mrs. Rickles looked like a wet dog, her hair was
flying in all directions as she slipped and fell down into the
muddy water, "Oh, shut up, Julie! If you were in control of your
stupid brats, things like this wouldn't happen!" And with that,
Mean Mrs. Rickles dove into the tussle with even more energy.
Jimmy was holding hard onto the back of Ryan's pants, pulling
him down into the water on top of himself. Ryan slipped down
the side of the ditch and began beating at the water, trying
to hit Jimmy. Jimmy was so outnumbered by the two crazy
Rickles that he was now scrambling, trying to get out of the
water as though he feared he might drown.

By now the neighbors were looking on from their backyards,
as the commotion had escalated. Dogs were barking up and
down the ditch line.

Her precious son, in his perfect little suit, was now muddy,
wet, screaming and crying as he flailed his arms at Jimmy,
who now was cowering against the ditch wall, protecting his
face from Ryan's wild blows.

Mean Mrs. Rickles was screaming in what sounded like a
strange language I had never heard before as she grabbed
Ryan's arm and twisted it away from Jimmy, who tried
unsuccessfully again to scratch his way up the muddy side
of the ditch to get away from both of them.

Mean Mrs. Rickles was screaming at the top of her lungs
and all of the boys were in stitches as I snapped picture
after picture until my camera beeped, indicating that it had
run to the end of a thirty-six picture roll.

Suddenly Mean Mrs. Rickles spun around and looked at me.

My camera was still trained on her and the boys in the ditch. 'OH, YOU THINK THIS IS SOME KIND OF A JOKE, DO YOU, BIRTHDAY BRAT? I SHOULD HAVE KNOWN BETTER THAN LETTING MY POOR RYAN COME TO A JUVENILE 'DELINQUENTS' HOUSE FOR THIS SAD EXCUSE FOR A PARTY! RYAN, YOU GET OUT OF THIS DITCH RIGHT NOW! WE ARE GOING HOME!'

Everyone stood there speechless, mostly me. I was so stunned that I still hadn't lowered my camera, which seemed to make Mean Mrs. Rickles even angrier.

My mom just stood there with her mouth hanging open as she looked down at Mean Mrs. Rickles, who was now soaked and muddy and screaming like a madwoman at everyone. It was weird, but my mom had both of her fists clenched.

I couldn't believe my luck. The biggest thing to happen in our neighborhood ever and I had it all on film.

Ryan and Mean Mrs. Rickles tried to claw their way out of the ditch, but she kept slipping back down into muddy brown water, getting totally soaked from her head down. She looked like a giant, soaked rat and Ryan was still sniffing and breathing hard.

Jimmy who had been cowering against the other side of the ditch finally climbed out the other side, away from the insane Rickles and was sitting on the concrete embankment near the street, wiping his bloody nose and probably trying to figure out how he would ever save face from this day.

Mean Mrs. Rickles and Ryan finally climbed out of the ditch, Ryan put both hands on her bottom from underneath hoisting her upward as she scratched and pulled, hanging onto the long weeds until she was up on the lawn. She gave everyone in the yard a look-that-kills look and started walking down the ditch, when she turned and spat at my mom, "DON'T YOU EVER SPEAK TO ME AGAIN! YOU BOYS SHOULD ALL BE ASHAMED OF YOURSELVES!" Then she bent down and whispered in Ryan's ear.

"NO WAY MOM!" he whined.

"GO! NOW!" his mother cackled like a Halloween witch.

Suddenly Ryan bolted away from her and ran back into my backyard. He went to the picnic table and grabbed the lame book he had brought for me as my birthday present and ran back to his mother's side.

"HE DOESN'T DESERVE IT!", she growled as they squish-squished their way down the ditch line toward their backyard. It was like the whole party and the whole neighborhood was holding its breath. The neighbors were now standing at their back fences in awe of what had just happened there.

When we heard the sound of the Rickles's loud, squeaking gate slam shut, my whole backyard broke into uncontrollable laughter, even my mom, though she still had a look of shock on her face. The laughter rolled down the ditch line from yard to yard until I am sure it reached the Rickles's house.

Nothing could ever top that for birthday party entertainment. We would talk about the details of the fight and of my birthday party for years to come.

CHAPTER TWENTY EIGHT

THE NIGHT WE MET THE VAMPIRE

At times I considered myself the dumbest kid on earth. I knew Carl could beat the tar out of me without even trying. He had a vicious temper and didn't think twice about punching me out, but I played practical jokes on him anyway.

One night when Andy couldn't sleep out in the tents because he was grounded for something, I decided to sleep in my room instead. Carl came into my room, threw himself down into the bottom bunk and stayed there.

I tried something new on him to scare him and to gross him out. I stuffed a wad of Black Jack gum into my mouth. There were five pieces in a pack, and my favorite way to eat them was a pack at a time. They turned my spit black, which made for really good drool.

Plus, Andy had showed me this trick. He'd acted like he'd been bitten by a vampire, putting drops of vampire blood on his neck. This blood was still red because he'd been human when he'd gotten bit. Then he'd chewed Black Jack gum, drooling it down his face, since blood turns black when you get bitten by a vampire.

Andy told me that when I got my brother's attention, I should be chewing the whole pack, and let a long string of black drool out. I should act like I were dying and was going to bite him next.

He said it worked every time.

Under the streetlight earlier I had noticed that several bats had been swooping after mosquitoes. Now, as I looked out my bedroom window, I saw what I thought was a monster bat swooping out there.

It would be scary for my big, fat, hairy, scary, dorky brother to think that a vampire had actually bitten me, so I made up this really cool story about it. While at dinner and when we were out playing hide-and-seek with the other kids, I kept telling Carl that I had gotten bit by a vampire and I could feel myself turning in to one. He just laughed it off nervously and called me all kinds of dumb names. But I could tell he was a little bit scared.

Later, as he was starting to fall asleep in his old bed, I leaned down into his space and said, "Did you see the bats hanging around here tonight?"

"NO!"

"They are under my command. I'm telling you..."

"Shut up. You are so weird."

"Seriously, gooooo assskkkk Mooommm... Do you want to hear a true scaaarrryyyy story?"

"NO!"

"Do you want to know why those bats are hanging around here?"

"NO! Gabe, I'm going to go back to my own room if you don't knock it off!"

But although neither of us would have admitted it, we wanted to have a sleepover like old times.

"Are you chicken?"

"NO!"

"Good. I've been waiting to tell you this totally true story for a couple days.

"Come on, Gabe, not again... I am really tired. Just go to sleep. I will go sleep in the tent if you are going to keep this up again."

"Oh, I wouldn't go out there if I were you."

"Why not?"

I started in with my scariest voice, "A week ago when the moon was full and we were sleeping out in the tent, I snuck out to sleep in the tree house. As I was climbing up the steps I heard the weirdest noise, a squeaking, screeching sound, and sitting right in the middle of the tree house was this giant, hairy, black bat... the size of a huge dog almost."

"Yeah, right! You expect me to believe that?"

"Go ask Moooommm..."

"You expect me to believe Mom knows about your dumb story this time? Do you think I am a total idiot."

I stayed totally quiet for a few minutes, letting Carl's imagination get the better of him. "Anyway, this bat lifted up, hovering mid-air three feet from the tree house floor. Suddenly, in a big puff of black smoke, it turned into this spooky-looking midget guy in a black cape. I started to laugh at him because he looked so funny, but he got really angry and jumped on me and started chewing on my neck."

'SHUT UP! THIS IS SO STUPID!'

I pushed my face into my pillow so I wouldn't laugh. I could tell he was getting kind of scared. That was the funny thing about Carl; though he was huge for his age and always acted so tough, he really was afraid of stuff, sometimes the dumbest stuff in the world. I could always tell if I was heading down a way that would scare him or if it was even too ridiculous for him.

'I was trying to fight him off, but his hand was like cold steel and I couldn't get it to budge off my neck. I passed out and woke up hours later. I was still up in the tree house, and several limbs above me was that same bat. He had blood on his mouth... my blood. On the way down out of the tree, I scraped my knee really badly, and on account of losing so much blood I got really dizzy and passed out again. I woke up just as the sun was coming up. I got this real sick feeling that I should get indoors before the sun rose. When I did, and looked at the blood on my knee, it was totally black, like a vampire's.'

'Chicken-freak, this is the lamest story I have ever heard. There's no such thing as vampires. You must think I am a total idiot to believe that story! You want me to think that you are some kind of vampire kid now? Give me a huge break.'

His voice was cracking.

'I do think you are a total idiot, but that's beside the point.'

He put his feet under my mattress and LAUNCHED me into the ceiling. 'Just SHUT UP and go to sleep.'

It hurt when my face hit the ceiling, but it made me even more determined to scare Carl. 'No can do. You have to hear the rest of what happened.' I slipped two pieces of the Black Jack gum into my mouth and chewed them, saving all of my spit. 'As I was saying when I looked at my knee, I saw that my blood had turned black the way it does when you get bitten by a vampire.'

'What's wrong with your mouth? You sound weird.'

'Ever since he bit me, my mouth has been freezing up! My tongue feels like a block of wood, and I'm always so cold...'

I slipped another piece of black Jack gum.

'COLD? It is like a sauna in here. How can you be cold?'

"When you have vampire blood coursing through your veins you are always cold until you get your next blood meal..."

"SHUT UP!"

I chewed on the other two pieces of Black Jack. There was so much spit in my mouth, I couldn't talk.

I dangled from the upper bunk into Carl's space, letting a huge dangle of black licorice drool spill onto his pillow right next to his face.

"WHAT THE HECK!"

I used my scariest vampire accent, "Blood is pouring from me, emptying me. I must have a blood meal..."

Carl jumped out of bed and turned on the light. My face must have been covered with the black "blood" because all of the blood drained out of his face upon seeing me. He looked at all of the "blood" on his pillow and freaked out, opening the door as he ran down the hall.

Mom and Dad were downstairs in the living room. I heard Mom call out, "Where are you going?"

"To sleep in the tent!"

I waited about ten minutes and then snuck down the stairs too. I slipped by without Mom or Dad seeing me, and went out into the backyard where Carl was trying to get some peace and quiet. I tiptoed across the street and climbed up into the tree house; it was only about thirty yards from where Carl was.

I started to make a scary howling sound. With just a little of the streetlight and the full moon lighting our backyard I could see Carl running back into the house. I wondered if he would sleep in the bathtub or in Mom and Dad's room.

All of a sudden it looked a lot darker up in the tree than it had just moments before. A cloud had moved over the moon. I looked up at where the moon had just been, and noticed the light from the streetlight shone on what looked like a big black bat right above my head.

With seconds I was frantically running through our back door and up the stairs to the safety of my own bedroom.

DEEDEN, REVISITED

On one of the last nights of summer as my brother slept I sneaked my little squirrel Deeden into his room. I had covered Deeden's mouth in vampire blood and superglued a couple of my baby teeth, that my mom keeps in a small box on my dresser, to look like fangs on him.

I turned on my brother's desk lamp to illuminate the little, rabid squirrel that I no longer needed to sleep with. I wasn't afraid of the dark anymore, but I wanted to make sure that Carl would continue to fear what crept down the hall and crept into his room in the middle of the night.

Since I had shared a room with Carl for so long, I knew he never slept through the entire night without either getting up to go to the bathroom or a glass of water. That night when he did, you could hear his "kindergarten-girl" scream all the way down the block.

When Carl came to pay me back, he found a pile of pillows under my blanket. I was sleeping like a baby in the bathtub behind the locked bathroom door.

THE MYSTERY OF THE CAVE MONSTER

Once Andy returned from his trip to New York we had to make up for lost time. We didn't have long before school was going to start, so we explored and played from morning to the night, slept mostly in my backyard tent and snuck around the neighborhood in the pitch black.

On the nights that were a little colder we would creep up to my room after raiding the fridge for midnight snacks and play monopoly or cards or just tell stories about the stuff we each did that summer when we were apart. A couple times I tried to talk to Andy about his dad, but he always changed the subject. I stayed away from it after that.

One day we went exploring near the railroad tracks right by Tunnel Number Two. There was a cliff with two small caves dug into it where Andy and I sometimes went to hang out when we wanted to make sure none of our brothers would find us. A tall, thick patch of mint was at the bottom of the cliff.

We were playing detectives when Andy slipped down the side of the cliff and landed in the mint patch. He was lying there groaning, acting like he was really hurt, even though he had only fallen about three feet. Then he flipped over on to his stomach and started yelling, "GABE! GET DOWN HERE!"

"What's wrong? Are you really hurt?" I slid down the cliff to where Andy was now scooting himself into the cliff. I could see that there was a small opening there. We both squeezed inside it.

"Wow, this is so cool!" I said.

"I've been down here a million times and didn't know this was here!"

"Me too!"

The cave went back about ten feet deep. There were several candy bar wrappers, some cigarette butts and a Coke can on the ground, so it was obvious someone else had discovered the cave before us.

We looked around for other clues. Up near the roof of the cave there were some weird-looking indentations on the wall and what looked like ancient carvings.

"Let's go get a flashlight!" I suggested.

We scooted out into the bright sunshine and headed for home.

"The Mystery of the Cave Monster!" Andy yelled, thinking about a similar title in our favorite mystery book series, The Happy Hollisters.

Andy and I were always exploring something. We had spent hours and hours at the dumps down by the railroad tracks finding all kinds of cool stuff from a long time ago, and we messed around in the basements of new houses that were being built collecting nails and other cool stuff the construction guys had thrown away. But we never knew of this cave with the cool secrets on its walls.

We were close to Andy's house when he said excitedly, "Maybe a treasure is buried somewhere around inside the cave, and that writing is a clue? Or maybe this is where criminals and hobos hide out?"

"Get your canteen and scout knife... I am going to pack a lunch."

"Okay!" I shouted. I headed for home, excited about what we might discover.

When I walked into the house Carl and Greg were sitting at the kitchen table having lunch.

"What are you all excited about, chicken-punk?"

"Don't call your brother a punk," Mom said for the millionth time.

"Nothing," I muttered, wondering how I was going to get away with packing a lunch and not letting on about our secret.

"Gabe, I made you a sandwich."

"I'll take it with me, Mom!"

I ran upstairs to get my gear. I stuffed my flashlight, canteen, pocketknife and some other supplies I thought might come in handy into my scout backpack. I went bounding down the stairs with my camouflage backpack over my shoulder.

"Where you going?" Carl sneered.

"None of your beeswax!" I sneered back, knowing I was safe from his punches with Mom so near. I ran downstairs to the bathroom to fill my canteen so Carl wouldn't see what I was doing. Then I ran back up the stairs to the kitchen.

"Mom, can I pack a whole lunch?"

"Sure, honey. Do you want some Oreos and chips to go with your sandwich?"

"Sounds great!"

"Sure, honey..." Carl whispered to Greg, "what a wussie..." He then changed voices and growled, "HEY, GABEY BABY, CAN WE COME WITH YOU?"

"Uh, no!"

"Where you going?" Greg asked, all polite-like so Mom would think he's a nice kid, which he was not!

Just then the doorbell rang. My dogs started going nuts, like they always did.

Carl took a long last drink from his coke and belched really loudly with a big "AH! Good lunch, Mom. Thanks!"

"Yeah, really, thanks Mrs. Peters," said Greg. He giggled at Carl's burp and punched his arm.

"Carl, where are your manners?" Mom scowled, but I could tell she was even impressed by the volume Carl could get with his burps by the way the sides of her mouth kind of smiled.

Mom handed me my lunch. I noticed she had put a big bag of carrot sticks in there, and a soda too. "Thanks, Mom!"

Andy stepped in. "Gabe! Are you ready?" He had his backpack on and hanging from his belt was a hatchet, canteen and a compass. He looked like he was ready for a month in the wilderness.

"Oh look, aren't they cute?" Carl laughed. "Are you little girls going on a little adventure today?"

Andy looked really self-conscious, but he was used to his four older brothers picking on him and could fire a good one back when a parent wasn't around. "Uh, not really. We thought we would walk down the railroad tracks and check out the skunk family, that's all."

"Oh, how sweet, the girls are going on a little adventure…"

"Just shut up, you dumb toad," I growled under my breath, loud enough for Carl to hear, but not Mom.

"MOM, CHICKEN-GABEY BABY SAID 'SHUT UP!'"

Mom just rolled her eyes. "You boys be careful not to go near them. Skunks can be very rabid."

"We won't, Mom. That's why Andy brought his binoculars. So we can see them from a good, safe distance." Andy had said what he did because it was in the opposite direction of where we were really going in case my dorky brother tried to follow us, like he and his friends always did.

We left the house, walking down the dirt road and then down a path in the field surrounded by tall yellow flowering weeds that were alive with bumblebees and gobs of grasshoppers. We headed toward the railroad track and then doubled back, hiding along the ditch until we reached the tree house right back across the street from my house.

We stayed up there until just a few minutes later, when Carl and Greg came bounding out of the house. Carl was practically shouting, "Okay, so we'll go up the barbwire fence and then cut down by the canyon where they say those skunks live."

"What do you want to do to them?"

"Let's really give them a scare!"

"Like what?"

"I dunno. Let's just follow them, spy on them and figure it out. Come onnnn! We gotta get a move on it. They have a good head start. We could lose them."

"Not the way your dumb brother walks! It will take him an hour just to get there with his leg."

Carl punched Greg on the arm hard. "I told you not to make fun of his leg!"

"He can't hear me! Jeez, you make fun of him all the time."

"NOT ABOUT THAT! JUST SHUT UP, GREG! I MEAN IT!"

"Jeez, Peters, you are so touchy." Greg followed behind Carl pouting.

It always made me feel weird when Carl stuck up for me like that, because I didn't usually like him, but when he did that it made me like him a lot — a whole lot.

They headed in the exact opposite direction of where we were going. Even if they doubled back and headed down the tracks where we were actually going to be, they would never see us because we would be inside the cave.

When we finally got back to the cave there were teenagers hanging around nearby, so we had to wait on the other side of the cliff, watching them with binoculars. They were smoking cigarettes. I wished I had my camera so I could send a picture to their moms in the mail and get them in some major trouble.

Andy suddenly shouted, "Hey, that's Johnny. What is he doing with those losers?"

I looked through his binoculars at Andy's brother John, who had arrived with his friend Cal from town. "Ohhh, look, he's smoking too."

"Oh man, Dad would skin Johnny if he saw that." The way Andy said that sent a chill up my spine.

We watched them for a long time, not saying a word. Finally the teenagers walked down to the tunnel, and we snuck down the cliff into the cave.

Andy scooted back to where we had seen the writing on the cave wall and flashed his flashlight on it. It was a drawing of what looked like the Indian from the legend Mr. Patchett had spoken of. It looked like the drawings had been there for a long, long time. Andy pulled out a sketchpad and started trying to imitate the drawing. "Your dad could take this to one of the scientists on the campus, couldn't he? These could be really, really old."

"Oh, yeah, Andy, but remember the last time we did that? It was embarrassing!"

"Yeah, but this could really be something this time!"

"Okay."

I wondered if this was the smartest idea. Even though Dad had thought it was a good way to learn last time, he might not be so amused to try again.

Last time Andy and I had gone on a mountain hike with our scoutmaster the previous summer. We had found a real cave, and all of us started exploring it. Andy and I climbed up on some huge boulders inside the cave and could see light coming through a huge crack. When we got to the crack we found these fist-size gemstones. We were convinced that we had happened on a cave full of valuable gems and would soon be very, very rich. We collected a whole bag of them, and my dad took them to the biology department on campus for testing by a geologist.

We even made up a paper stating that the scientists would keep our find totally secret until we could get the rights to mine the gems in the cave in the national forest. We made it look all legal-like, copying it to look the same way as a legal paper my dad had, with a place for the scientists to sign it and everything.

About a week later dad came home with a very official-looking document on the college letterhead and everything. It said: This is to inform you that testing had been conducted on your discovery from the national forest cave. Although it is not valuable, it is an interesting find. What you have is petrified bat guano. We would appreciate it if you could give us map coordinates so some of our mineralogists could further explore the cave. Thank you for your contribution to science.

All that week, Andy and I had drawn up paper after paper about what we were going to do with our millions of dollars from what we thought was a black diamond mine, and all it was the whole time was ancient bat poop. I had never been more humiliated in my life.

We sat in the cave talking about the cavemen who might have lived in this cave and how this cave had been here through the whole history of time. I wondered if any of the hobos that we had seen riding the train had ever found it and made a home in it until it was time to move on. I even imagined cowboys sleeping in the cave as Indians were in pursuit, as well as so many other possibilities. We made up a ton of stories when suddenly above us there were voices.

I could hear Carl talking to Greg, "Johnny said he saw them down here."

"Well, they aren't here anymore."

They started skipping rocks off of the cliff, plunking them into the stream flowing just yards away from the cave. We eavesdropped on their conversation, hoping for something that we could get them in trouble for later. They just talked about dumb stuff and pretended they were in the army on some mission. Those dummies had two games they played: baseball and army.

They played on the cliffs for a long time while we waited for them to leave, so we were stuck in the cave.

In the meantime Andy and I decided that we would look in the books in the library for similar cave drawings to see if these really were old like the ones they found in Egypt. We wanted to make sure this time before we were the laughing stock on the college campus again.

As we waited for Carl and Greg to leave, a new monster story started to form in my mind. It was about a cave monster who crept out of his cave at night, roaming around our neighborhood looking for big, hairy, scary, dorky, stinky big brothers, one that would definitely scare Carl enough to send him to Mom and Dad's room or at least the bathtub. This time I would tell Mom the whole story first, and time it so when I tried to convince Carl that it was true, I would say, "Go assssskkkk Mooooommm" and then would immediately call her into the room so she could chime in. I think she would do it since she saw how mean he was to me all the time.

Finally Carl and Greg gave up and started heading back to the neighborhood, where no doubt they would torment some other younger brothers.

"Well, day after tomorrow it's back to school, dang it!" Andy growled in a whisper to make sure my brother couldn't hear us.

"It's getting chilly. It's probably time to get going."

"Yeah, Hey Peters..."

"Yeah?"

"You're my best friend."

"Yeah, I am."

We locked arms around each other's shoulders and headed for home.

From outside the cave, I could have sworn I heard the monster exhale.

OUR BUNK BED DAYS ARE OVER

Well, I never in a million years thought that having my own room would make me happy and sad, but the truth was, as strange as it may sound, I missed my brother. I left the bunk beds up in my room for sleepovers with friends, but even more because of the nights Carl would come in and flop down on his bunk like he was doing me some huge favor by hanging out in there with me. It's funny; we both liked that a lot, but neither one of us would have ever said it out loud.

There was a time when I would have done anything to escape sleeping in the upper bunk because of Carl's launches, or something else mean, but there were also those occasional warm summer nights when the crickets were cheeping and a soft breeze would waft into our room when Carl wasn't in a totally bad mood that we would talk about real stuff that was on our minds. We talked about all kinds of things we both usually just kept in our heads, knowing somehow that talking like this was a special thing, one we would never share with another human being.

It was on those rare occasions that I caught glimpses of a friendship that would bloom between me and Carl decades later.

Sometimes Carl and I talked about what we wanted to be when we grew up. Sometimes we just joked around or had a farting contest, and laughed so hard we would rock the bed. The night before school was going to start, I was really uneasy about starting in another school. Mom and Dad had decided that I would be better off in the school the other kids in our neighborhood went to so I wouldn't always feel left out. I also felt bad because I was repeating fourth grade, which is a long story in itself. I could tell Carl was kind of nervous about going to Junior High. He crept into my room and asked if he could sleep in his old bed.

"Sure."

"No stories," he growled.

"Okay."

He climbed into his old bed. I found the spot on the ceiling that always looked like a little old lady to me. "Hey Carl, you remember that insane guy..."

"Gabe, I'm serious. I don't want to hear about it."

"Okay, did you hear the one about the wallpaper hanger with only one arm?"

And so it went. I told him funny stories until we were both cracking up. It was funny. Sometimes I thought I hated Carl more than anything, but I would do anything for him, too. He had stood up for me all summer when the kids were really mean, and even though he never said it, I knew he deep down inside liked me too.

"Hey Carl..." I waited for him to answer but he didn't. "You're a good big brother..." I whispered.

The sound of his snores echoed off the bottom of the upper bunk.

Summer was over. School was beginning again, and I was switching schools and repeating the fourth grade. I would finally get to ride the big yellow school bus with all of the other "normal" kids who went to the public school. This time there would be no Sister Mary Claire, the meanest nun to ever teach in an elementary school classroom, because I was going to go to the regular school.

The good news was that my leg was stretching out and Doctor Rumley told me that within a year I wouldn't have to wear a special shoe to school anymore. Also, Mom came through with her promise and let me ditch the huge black-framed glasses for a much cooler pair of wires. My lazy eye was getting stronger too, and Doctor Rumley thought I would outgrow most of it and that the patch I wore when it got really bad could come off for good.

So I was heading into new territory. The kids at the new school didn't think I was as big of a geek, because they didn't know me, except for the kids from my neighborhood, and most of them were my friends anyway. Plus it didn't hurt that the older kids were all really afraid of my big brother, who was now a big, tough Middle Schooler.

See you next summer!

EPILOGUE

The summer Carl and I came back home for a family reunion, our three sons slept in our old room, the two older on the bunk beds. Carl and I slept out under the stars in the backyard where our tent had been pitched every summer on the very first day out of school. Our shared experiences as boys in the country neighborhood were clouded by the passage of time now, as we were surrounded by carpet stores and car dealerships in what used to be backyards and grassy fields.

We talked about the kids we had grown up with, wondering whatever became of Tyler and Kevin. The last we'd heard about them was that Kevin had spent some time in a juvenile detention home. Those poor kids never had a chance with a dad like theirs.

Carl had kept in touch with some of the old neighborhood buddies for a while after high school, but when he moved to California he lost touch with everyone, except me, of course.

Still, even with all that had built up around the old Skyview neighborhood, the sound of frogs across the street in the pond and the crickets hiding in the grass was a reminder of those simple days.

I looked across the street, and above the pond in the tree was the floor of what had once been quite a tree house. I knew I would take my sons up into it the next day and tell them stories about how I spied once on the little old lady who lived up on the hill. Maybe I would even tell them about my first kiss, which had happened in that same tree house where I spent so many hours of my boyhood.

Sometime around midnight Carl nudged my arm.

"Hey Gabe, wake up."

"Huh?"

"You wanna go down to the lake?"

"What?"

"Let's go down the lake like we used to when we were kids."

"Why?"

"I dunno. Maybe we will finally see the dead dog at the bottom?"

We walked barefoot down familiar streets, which now seemed so much narrower than I remembered them, past Mercury, Mars, and The Milky Way. My feet were tender now and felt every stone in the newly-paved streets that, when I was still a boy, were just gravel and dust. I remembered that my feet used to be so tough with calluses that they felt like thick leather.

The familiar scent of the swampy water hit my nose, and near the small dock was a rowboat, turned over in the weeds. We pushed the boat into the water and began to row toward the middle, both of us armed with flashlights.

"Say, Carl, remember the night old man Patchett pulled us out of the lake and called Dad?"

"He always had it out for me..."

"What about Mean Mrs. Rickles?"

"Oh man, don't get me started..."

We laughed and shared stories as the rowboat lazily drifted around the lake. I was amazed at how different Carl's memories were from mine.

"Shoot," he said, "we should have brought the boys down here. There's nothing like this in the city."

"Yeah, but Carl, it's kind of nice just being here with you."

"Hey Gabe, remember you were always writing in those diaries and journals of yours when we were kids? You ought to read them and write a book about all that stuff. I know my boys like those stories, and man, their lives are so different than ours were."

"Hmmm, maybe I will... Hey look, Old Man Patchett's back porch light just came on. You don't think..."

From down the canyon a bird called, "Iiiiiseeeeeyouuuuuu."